Golden Handcuffs Review

Golden Handcuffs Review Publications

Seattle, Washington

Golden Handcuffs Review Publications

Editor

Lou Rowan

Contributing Editors

Andrea Augé
Nancy Gaffield
Peter Hughes
Stacey Levine
Rick Moody
Toby Olson
Jerome Rothenberg
Scott Thurston
Carol Watts

Layout management by Pure Energy Publishing, Seattle
PUREENERGYPUB.WORDPRESS.COM

Libraries: *this is Volume II, #32*

Information about subscriptions, donations, advertising at:
www.goldenhandcuffsreview.com

Or write to: Editor, Golden Handcuffs Review Publications
1825 NE 58th Street, Seattle, WA 98105-2440

In Memory,
Michael Spafford
1935 - 2022

Contents

THE WORK

Art

Michael Spafford
> #24 from Iliad, 2004 (top)
> #1 from Iliad, 2004 (bottom) .... cover

Fiction

Brian Marley
> from the novel *Crime, My Destiny* 9

Stacey Levine
> from *Mice 1961* 51

George Salis
> The Infant King 89

Poetry

Fanny Howe
> Cryptic 7

Kat Peddie
> Three Poems 26

Nancy Gaffield
> Three Poems 35

Ralph Hawkins
> Seven Poems 41

Ron Silliman
> from *Now, Here, This: Half-Sonnets* 48

Norman Fischer
> from *Men in Suits* 70

Hank Lazer
from *Three Four Five* and *Pieces* 77

Lee Duggan
from *Residential Poems* 83

Jesse Glass
Three Poems 108

Prose Poetry

John Olson
Eight Prose Poems 31

Interview

Charles Bernstein, Pierre Joris, Habib Tengour
Three Poets in New York 60

RESPONSE

Ian Brinton
Growing Dumb: An Autobiography of an English Education
by Peter Quartermain 22
The Blue Split Compartments by Andrea Brady 56

Toby Olson
Carol Watts' Poetry 120

John Olson
Telling Time, A review of Rosemarie Waldrop's
The Nick of Time 124

NOTES ON CONTRIBUTORS 128

Cryptic

Fanny Howe

Okay Ruby
It's time
We're leaving home
Red eyed and blue.

Click on a shadow
And your mother dies.
Line up your claws
Where your master waits.

Inside an egg there is equidistance
The way it is for us
Feathers and beaks
Drilling a hole to see a star millions of miles off.

Seaweed from the mighty Shannon floor
Is as green as an early acorn.
Wrap my grenade in lettuce
Then and play the fife and drum.

Under-war forms of metal
Last until the top is loosed
How long does gladness
Keep light alive?

To die as a premonition
Never known to the gods.
You must give away your possessions.
Lie flat and close your eyes. Something always happens.

Are you dead yet my bad friend
Only yards away. I think there are clusters
Of people born together forever.
But they don't know it until they can't.

from the novel
Crime, My Destiny

Brian Marley

In the months that followed I managed, with difficulty, to broker two or three vehicles a week from Portfolio A – the "poor-man's-plenty" models, as Joe had dubbed them – but none of the posh cars from Portfolio Z. My heart wasn't in it, and Billy/2 and Frank were, to say the least, disappointed by my lacklustre performance. They grumbled and swore and made increasingly threatening noises. They said [*I'm paraphrasing here, dialing it down for readers of faint heart and fluttery pulse*] that things couldn't go on as they were and I'd better pull my socks up or woe betide. Besides which, I was no longer earning enough to put food on the table, never mind pay my share of the rent. To make ends meet I'd been borrowing heavily from Billy/2 at an astronomical rate of interest.

The punters seemed happy, though. They were each getting a jolly good car, real value for money, and if it was their preference to buy from a "private owner" rather than a dealer, well, that's what I said I was, and that Ben, who would deliver the car to them, was my brother-in-law. Little white porkies, where's the harm in that? But the idyll was well and truly over.

I didn't feel the blow that knocked me off my feet. Nor did I see it coming. After a moment of confusion, during which I may have lost consciousness, I found myself face down in an alleyway off Peter Street. Because my shirt and vest were rucked up under my armpits, I assumed I'd been assaulted at or near the mouth of the alley and dragged here feet first. One side of my head felt like it was on fire, and the blood – most definitely blood – that was seeping into my ear tickled and tormented me. I wanted to rub it away but couldn't because my wrists were secured behind my back by something cold and metallic – handcuffs (RMP issue, I later discovered). My ankles, roughly bound with what felt like garden twine, had been drawn up in a tight bow and tethered to my wrists. I could wriggle like an eel and rock from side to side but movement of almost any other kind was impossible. In addition to which, someone was straddling my upper torso, making it hard for me to breathe.

When a voice hissed in my other ear, I knew immediately who it was and my heart sank. "Am I angry?" said old Bushell in rhetorical mode – a first for him. First and last, as it turned out. "No, I'm damned angry. The cars you sell are crooked cars and you sell them in a crooked manner. Your disregard for the rule of law offends me, and if, God forbid, to add to his woes, your father were to learn that this is what you're doing to earn a crust, he'd be mortified. Given his heart condition, it could finish him off. You're not half the man he is, you maggot. But worse than that, worse by far, is that for no reason other than perverse self-gratification you ambushed my boy and killed him stone dead. No, don't try to deny it!"

Frankly, I was in no fit state to do anything of the sort. And I was astonished: never before had I heard Bushell Senior utter more than six words at a time, none of which extended beyond two syllables. For years, during office hours, he'd been limiting himself to only the shortest and most obsequious words in his lexicon. I admit, I almost felt sorry for him, until he said, "I could kill you now. Easily done. But I won't make your parents mourn as I do. Once they've passed on, that's when I'll finish you off. In the meantime you'll suffer grievously, doubt be damned. I'll kill you one nick at a time, and when the first cut shows signs of healing I'll inflict another, then another, each a little nastier than the one before. I'll rub a salve of ground glass and rat droppings into the wounds until they fester. You'll be kept not just in constant pain but in an agony of anticipation.

Old I may be, but don't get your hopes up; I'll send the Grim Reaper packing with a flea in his ear until the death of my beautiful boy, Junior Bushell, has been avenged."

That's when I realised that Junior's first name was actually Junior. Yes, *Junior.* It had never occurred to me to question what was on his birth certificate; I'd just assumed it was Beaumont or Peregrine, Hercules or Wolf, something fusty and/or ludicrous, something the school bullies would pounce on with unmitigated glee.

I was still mulling this over when the pressure on my chest suddenly eased. Raising my head as best I could, I watched my assailant stroll to the mouth of the alley and turn left into Soho's hivelike bustle, apparently without a care in the world, and I couldn't help but wonder: What was his first name? Surely not Mister … But really, the whole Bushell family was downright weird, so who knows?

The first person to find me had entered the alley specifically to urinate behind a stack of crumpled cardboard boxes. Decorum personified; thousands of years of social evolution had led to this moment. He looked me over with casual disdain as I lay there, almost at his feet, bleeding from a head wound and trussed up like an oven-ready turkey. Once his bladder had been thoroughly drained, he shook off the last few drops and buttoned up his flies. Hunkering down beside me he said, "Dear-o-deary me. Looks like you're in a spot of bother, old chum." "Yes," I replied. *I mean, really, what else could I say?* Then I thought of something: "Might I trouble you to untie me? I'd be ever so grateful." He rocked back on his heels while he considered my request then shook his head. "Nah, 'fraid not. Too risky. You might decide to cut up rough while I'm rummaging about your person."

Which is what he then set about doing.

Having relieved me of my wallet, wristwatch, hat and shoes, he tried to pull my trousers down, reason unknown. His efforts, though vigorous, failed because of how tightly bound I was. "Bit of a snag," he said, panting from his exertions. "I think, under the circumstances, that's all the help I can give you, good samaritan that I am. Have a nice day as our American cousins say. Bye now."

No sooner had he departed than a tall fellow wearing a black borsalino and a bulky astrakhan coat, also black, glanced into the alley, did a double take and stood there, squinting into the shadows, trying to work out whether his eyes were deceiving him – which, of course, they weren't. He took a few steps towards me, hesitant still, then his face lit up. "Well, well, well," he said. "As I live and breathe. Just the man I was looking for."

I had no idea who he was, though there was something vaguely familiar about him.

"It is Charles W————, isn't it?" he said. "Indeed it is. I'd have recognised you anywhere, even in the bashed-up state you're in. You look just like the photo the tabloids like best: the choirboy shot. Were I asked to caption it, I'd say, right off the top of my head, 'Innocence masking depravity'. Not bad, eh? I've still got the knack. I wanted to be a caption writer when I grew up, as do most public schoolboys of a literary bent, especially those influenced by Papa Hemingway's lean and muscular prose style, but a strong dose of fatherly advice set me on a different career path. Not that I gave up on caption writing entirely, you understand, but I didn't pursue it professionally, and perhaps, given how poorly remunerated it is, that's no bad thing. Anyway, the choirboy photo has no need of words. It's a picture editor's wet dream, perfect in itself.

"Speaking of newspapers, I don't know whether you had time to flick through today's early edition of the *Standard* before" – he indicated my trussed-up torso with an eloquent sweep of his hand – "this happened, but there's good news. You've been relegated to page five, and what the poor misguided reader will find there is nothing but tittle-tattle, barrel scrapings. Soon you'll disappear from its pages entirely and I'd lay odds you can't wait for that to happen. The bad news is they're still saying you murdered that poor mite, which is troubling because you and I know better.

"But really, what must you think of me? Although I climbed out of bed on the sunny side this morning, I seem to have left my manners dozing on the eiderdown. Allow me to introduce myself. The name's Pew, Norbert Pew, though my friends at temple call me Khufu. You, I think, are Redjedef – am I right?" He proffered a hand for me to shake, then blushed. "Of course. What a Grade-A ninny I am. Let me release you, it'll only take a sec."

I wondered whether, in my dazed condition, I'd misheard him. How could he possibly know that Father had called me Redjedef?

And as for the comment about my innocence ...

Taking a small penknife from his trouser pocket, he angled out its comically stubby blade by 180° and used it to sever the twine at my wrists and ankles – whereupon my legs uncoiled like overwound springs and my unshod feet crashed to the ground, toes first, pounding the concrete like

[*uh-oh, one simile too many*]

ten tiny hammers. Pain shot through me like

[*a third, and in swift succession – I dread to think what Lupin will say*]

an electric current and I gave a loud, girlish shriek. "Oh, my dear boy!" he said. "Terribly sorry!" Then: "Nothing to be done about the handcuffs for the moment, but I know for a fact that the hardware store round the corner sells bolt cutters, and as the owner is an old schoolpal of mine – my one-time fag, in fact, at Marlborough, though he says he bears me no ill-will because I treated him more like a pet, a dumb animal, than a servant or a slave – I'm sure he'll get those cuffs off pronto, no questions asked."

To make the handcuffs less conspicuous, he draped his coat over my shoulders, though my bloodied head and lack of shoes drew quizzical glances anyway. Everyone who saw me knew who I was, of course. They'd been avidly reading newspaper reports about the ongoing manhunt and probably thought I'd been nabbed by a bounty hunter, though Pew didn't really look the part.

As we staggered along (I was woozy, unsteady on my feet, and my toes had swollen to twice their usual size), Pew hooked his arm through mine, for support, and something clicked into place, jigsaw fashion. I realised where I'd seen him before: The Luxor Temple, and on more than one occasion. When he mentioned having "friends at temple", I'd assumed he meant synagogue. Not so. If he was who I think he was, he always sat with his back to the wall, sipping whisky and scanning the room in a propriatorial manner.

At the store, Pew's pal snipped off the cuffs, snip-snip, no fuss. He gently sponged the worst of the blood from my head, then applied sticking plasters to the alley-drag scuffs on my brow, nose and chin. Meanwhile, Pew went to a pharmacy to buy aspirin and a mile or two of crepe bandage. Having had my wound dressed turban-style, I gulped down a handful of pills, donned a pair of white slaughterman's wellington boots (the only footwear the store had in stock that could accommodate my swollen toes), and we set off to the nearest pub.

While Pew busied himself at the bar, I slumped into a cosy nook by the fire, and when he brought the drinks over I said, in as threatening a tone as I could manage, "You said you were looking for me, Mr Pew. You're not a reporter, I hope. If you are –"

He chuckled. "Dear Lord, no. What a horrible idea. No, I'm here to relay confidential information about the late Joseph Qureshi, your erstwhile friend and employer and my erstwhile business partner ... Which means in effect that you're now, or pretty soon will be, my business partner."

"*What?* How d'you reckon that, then?"

"Brace yourself," he said. "This may come as a shock, albeit a pleasant one. Joseph left you a quarter share in The Luxor Temple."

I laughed. Couldn't help myself. "Go on. You're winding me up. He did nothing of the sort."

"I assure you, he did."

"There's no will, Mr Pew –"

"Khufu, please."

"– Joe died intestate, that's a fact. There – is – no – will. Paula and I looked everywhere."

"Everywhere but in the right place," he said, "by which I mean the extensive documents vault in the basement of Rosewart, Sample and Pew – the Pew in that short list being my twin brother Adrian, a junior partner in the firm and Rosewart's most put-upon dogsbody. Ade was tasked with delivering the good news about the will, but as there wasn't a current address for you on file, you being a fugitive and all, he hadn't a clue where to begin. Being savvier than him, more streetwise, and with an extensive network of underworld contacts to draw on, I did, and told him so, whereupon, visibly relieved, he delegated the task to me. 'Strictly hush-hush, Bert,' he said. 'Don't let Rosewart know I haven't done it in person. He's very touchy about his delegatees palming a task off on someone else, especially if that someone isn't a Rosewart employee. But if you do happen to find this Charles W—————— character, which, given your admirable track record, I'm sure you will, there's a bottle of Krug in my cellar with your name on it.'

"Therefore," said Pew, spreading his arms wide, as if to encompass not just the pub but Soho and perhaps the whole wide world, "here I am, your humble delegatee. I suppose you could say I'm Rosewart's dogsbody's unofficial dogsbody."

He laughed as though he'd said something funny, then his facial muscles relaxed more than one would have thought possible, which made him look like he was melting.

"Joseph was buried more than three months ago, God rest his soul, so I'm sure you're wondering: Why the delay? I'll tell you why. An administrative error is why. Human error, to be precise. A junior clerk who sorely neglected his Ps and Qs and thought I before E except after C was how filing was done in the legal profession. Not precisely that but something close. Straight out of boarding school so he was bound to know no better. Anyway, chaos ensued, as you can imagine. Although Joseph's will was known to be in the vault, it couldn't be found. Such things happen in even the best-regulated businesses. They shouldn't but they do.

"Apparently, Rosewart instructed Ade to tender his, i.e. Rosewart's, apologies. Sincere and profound ones, of course; nothing but the best for you. Consider it done, and expect to receive complimentary grand tier tickets to the Royal Opera House once I, via Ade, have notified Rosewart's secretary of your current place of abode. Rosewart may also invite you to dine at his home in Sidcup with the delectable Mrs Rosewart. Almost certainly, in fact. It's standard procedure: damage limitation. He'll feel the need to schmooze you, fearful lest you lodge a complaint with the Law Society or try to sue him for negligence.

"Should you wish to pursue the latter option I would, of course, be delighted to represent you, pro bono. Here, take this." He drew a business card from his wallet and flipped it onto the table. When it landed face down, he sighed, turned it over and slid it towards me, narrowly avoiding a small puddle of beer. It read: Layman, Bancroft, Treddle and Pew. "That's me," he said unnecessarily, jabbing his surname with a long, bony forefinger. "Though last on the list, I'm the boss."

He then produced another card. "Adrian's phone number,"

he explained. "You'll need to book an appointment with him, to sign a few documents. Various legal hoops have to be jumped through to satisfy all parties. That goes for your girlfriend, too."

"Paula?"

"Indeed. Unless you've been a naughty boy, playing away from home, which as everyone in Soho knows – because everyone in Soho knows almost everything about everyone else in Soho, *as well you know* – you haven't. Probably haven't. So, yes, Miss Cantabile. Joseph was inordinately fond of her and she of him. She's to receive a quarter share in the Temple, same as you. I'm the fifty-percenter, Joseph's sleeping partner as was, now wide awake and raring to go. Let's not beat about the bush, Charles: I want to buy you out, both of you, and at a premium. Think about it. Think hard. It's a serious proposition. You're in dire financial straits right now, I know you are, everyone says so, and things can only get worse if you remain in hock to Bill Wainscott. He's a bad man even by gangland standards. And don't think he's unaware of what you and Joe were getting up to behind his back. He'll punish you for that, and not just with the hyper-inflationary vig on your loan.

"Consider it this way: the wherewithal from selling your share of the Temple would enable you to pay him off and get out from under his thumb. If you don't, sooner or later he'll crush you like the veritable bug. Every one of his employees eventually gets crushed or jailed. Or worse. Given Frank Blatchington's laziness and disgusting sexual habits, it's remarkable that he's lasted as long as he has. Perhaps Wainscott cuts him some slack because he enjoys being adored.

"I don't know whether you know it, but Wainscott's previous consigliere, if that's the right term, Linton Eakins, who was once a celebrity wedding photographer, ended up quartered in a holdall under Tower Bridge. Though the Met searched high and low, his head and legs were never found.

"But let's not dwell on unpleasantness, eh? This is a good-news day! Let's have another drink to celebrate. In fact, as it's cosy in here and your head has almost stopped bleeding, let's make a session of it. Afterwards we can trot over to Veeraswamy for a slap-up meal. My treat, what do you say?"

"Sorry, Mr Pew, I can't."

"Why ever not? And please call me Khufu. It's an excellent

curry house, the first of its kind in old London town and still ranked among the best."

"So I've heard. And I appreciate your kind offer. The problem is it's on the far side of Regent Street, outside the safety zone. If I leave Soho I'll be at risk of getting nicked."

"Ah. Ah-ah-ah-ah-ah. So it is and so you could. Which rules out the Opera House and Sidcup too, doesn't it? And even the trip to Rosewart's office, which is over by Marble Arch. I'd better let Adrian know what's what and why so he can brief Rosewart about your travel restrictions, otherwise Rosewart will commit a faux pas and lay the blame on Ade, something The Wart – his nickname, even his wife calls him that – has a habit of doing.

"I don't know why Ade puts up with Rosewart's hectoring manner, really I don't. Were it not for the fact that Ade and I are identical twins, with similar haircuts and a tendency to dress alike, I'd hire him like a shot. He's got a sound legal mind. He'd be an asset to the firm. Admittedly, unless we took to wearing colour-coded ties, it would be confusing for everyone but ourselves – the 'twinny twosome', as our parents fondly called us, shortly before skiing into the path of an avalanche that swept them down the mountain and out of our lives – and life is confusing enough as it is. Also, Ade probably wouldn't be happy playing second fiddle. He's a go-getter, future driven, an underdog striving to be top dog, and the fact that he's my younger brother, even if only by a minute or so, means he looks up to me and always has done, though he also resents and probably hates me. We'd end up squabbling like children, as we did when we actually were children.

"Hmm ... On second thoughts, hiring Ade would be a bad idea. Terrible, in fact. But as everyone knows, good ideas follow bad, hot on their heels, so ... what'll it be, Charles, another Guinness?"

✳

After a further half hour of Pew's self-regarding tosh, there was nothing I wanted more than to be rid of him. When I was finally able to get a word in edgeways, I explained that not only was my head throbbing fit to burst, I also had double vision. I said I appeared to be sitting opposite not just him but Adrian too, each identical to the other down to the minutiae – all-but-invisible soup stains on ties and lapels, etc.

They nodded sympathetically, in sync.

What would be best for me, I said, would be to go home and straight to bed, to rest and recuperate.

Pew recognised a snub when he heard one and to his credit he took it in his stride. He said he hoped I'd make a full and speedy recovery from the blow to my head, which was undoubtedly the cause of my double vision, given that my alcohol intake had been, by any fair reckoning, meagre, and it was common knowledge that I wasn't an habitual drunk – something, alas, that couldn't be said of my Devonian pal Billy, an alcoholic in all but name and a disruptive influence on everyone who so much as bumped elbows with him.

To expedite my departure – or Pew's, it didn't matter to me which of us made the first move – I chose to ignore his assassination of Billy's character, though it rankled. And because I was mindful to mind my manners, I thanked him for all he'd done for me. I said, through gritted teeth, that without his timely intervention I might still be lying in that alley, gnawed to the bone by rats, Soho rats, said to be even more ferocious than the so-called psycho-rats bred at the Ministry of Defence's Defence Science and Technology Lab, otherwise known as Porton Down, where the psychos, as part of a top-secret toxic weapons programme, were being trained to undertake kamikaze-style missions behind enemy lines in order to teach various jumped-up Johnny Foreigner nations a swift, salutory lesson, one they'd be unlikely to forget in a hurry.

I have no idea where that came from.

Pew was stunned. Temporarily lost for words. Then, "Oh, tush," he said. What he meant by that I have no idea. He pumped my hand vigorously and departed in a swirl of Canoe Dana cologne.

Although I'd had every intention of following in his slipstream, I found myself lard-arsed (or if, as a descriptor, you prefer soft metal to rendered pig fat: leaden-arsed), i.e. unable to move. My mind was in turmoil and I felt foolishly near to weeping. It had been a day chock-full of surprises, most of them unpleasant, the nastiest one of all being the violent encounter with Mr Bushell. More of a shock than a surprise, really. No, let's not pussyfoot: *very much more!* It had simply never occurred to me that he'd try to track me down. But now that he'd done so I knew, without a shadow of a doubt, that he intended to kill me as specified.

Nor, for that matter, while trussed up and unable to defend myself, had I enjoyed being stripped of my valuables. The wristwatch in particular. It had been Father's and, prior to that, Grandfather's, and etched on its back was a hieroglyph. I have no idea what the glyph signified. Not a clue. I'd never tried to find out and now ... well, now it was too late. But what I do know is that if I'd shown even the slightest interest in the glyph, Father would have expatiated on its meaning and significance till the cows come home, and ... bear with me, this is a bit of a stretch ... the info he'd imparted might be of use to me now in extricating myself from the mire in which I was chin deep and in danger of drowning.

Talk about clutching at straws!

What can I say? That's how desperate I was.

Also puzzled. Particularly when, in introducing himself, Pew called me Redjedef. What was I to make of that? He must have overheard, or somehow gained knowledge of, the private conversation I'd had with Father about metempsychosis and our family's Egyptian heritage. Royal ancestry among the ancients, no less. But ... how?

Then came the news that I would soon become part-owner of The Luxor Temple. Although Joe's bequest was a blessing and had obviously been intended as such, it felt like ... not a curse exactly. To think of it in that way would be an insult to Joe's memory and an exaggeration, the kind of figurative language I strenuously avoid, as the more perceptive readers among you will already have noted.

But really, what did I know about running a highly successful private members' club such as The Luxor Temple? Nothing. Not a sausage. Not even a quarter of a sausage.

It was too much to take in. Too unsettling. I consoled myself with the thought that if I didn't die in my sleep from a massive brain bleed everything would look different tomorrow, less confusing, less bleak. Better, in other words. One can only hope.

Also, I wondered why Pew hadn't asked me whether I knew my assailant. It seemed an obvious question and an odd omission, especially for a lawyer, and especially with regard to Soho where, as Pew himself had pointed out, almost everyone knows everyone else, fellow residents mainly but also dozens of regular visitors, some for work, some to play.

When I finally managed to exit the pub it was with no clear destination in mind. I placed one foot doggedly in front of the other, oblivious to my surroundings, and all the while disquieting thoughts raced madly through my head, bouncing off the walls of my skull and crashing into each other like bees in dodgem cars.

Bees? I hear you ask. *Bees?*

Zig-zag flight, flower to flower.

Dodgems is self-explanatory.

Do try to keep up.

So unsteady was I in my loose-fitting slaughterman's boots that I was bound to come a cropper eventually – and so I did, hours later, under harsh neon light, outside Club Papa Pistolet. As I finished crossing Berwick Street (having narrowly avoided being knocked into next week by a recklessly driven Morris Minor, one I'd brokered from Portfolio A, easily distinguishable from all the other Morris Minors on the road by its polka-dot paint job), the heel of my leading boot snagged the kerb and I was sent sprawling into the club's recessed doorway, banging my head hard against the door itself, which swung open, juddering on its hinges.

Disoriented though I was, when I saw the bar, brightly lit at the end of a long, dark corridor, I realised that during my lengthy meanderings around Soho I'd developed a veritable Atacama of a thirst.

The place had been quite amusing when I'd visited it several weeks ago with Frank, when we were still on good terms, so I decided to look in on its cheerful host, Luigi Caputo, a Weegie in exile, formerly a hatchet man for the Calton Tongs and, while barely out of short pants, a razor boy, or so he claimed. Altogether a dangerous fellow if you crossed him but also an exceptionally gifted raconteur. Luigi was said to possess the most wittily waspish tongue in all of Soho: entertainment guaranteed! Perhaps cruel verbal barbs sunk deep into the piggy hide of various politicians and stars of stage and screen would make me forget my troubles, at least for an hour or two.

Because of having been mugged, I was, of course, strapped for cash, but as Luigi and I had hit it off during my previous visit I felt confident that he would, when he saw the sorry state I was in, allow me to put a beer or two on Frank's tab if I promised to square it with him later. Preferably sooner than later. I had no intention of doing anything of the sort but Luigi wasn't to know that. Frank was now my mortal enemy. I owed him nothing but contempt. He –

What the –? Is that what I think it is?

Car wheels crunching on the gravel driveway, faint at first but getting louder. Sound of a braking skid followed by the loud tick-tick-tick of an engine starting to cool down, just below my window, which I'd thrown open to capture the warm summer breeze. A car door slammed. Ditto, seconds later, the house door. Suddenly Lupin was in the room with me, bristling with anger. She threw her coat against the wall and said, or rather yelled, "The deal's off!"

"Eh? What deal's that, then?"

"The one with Aardman, you idiot! The big one that was supposed to make our fortune and get us out of this poxy cottage in the middle of bloody nowhere and into a nice Regency townhouse in Soho where you'd be safe from arrest and I could host a literary salon – you know, readings from books on the eve of publication by the authors of said books, famous authors reading to equally famous authors: Man Booker Prize winners, Crime Writers' Association Daggers Award winners, Costa Book Prize winners, Women's Prize for Fiction winners, International Dylan Thomas Prize winners, Jhalak Prize winners, James Tate Black Memorial Prize winners, British Book Award winners, Walter Scott Prize for Historical Fiction winners, even Goldsmiths Prize winners – all winners, nothing but winners, no long- or even short-listers and certainly no riff-raff unless they're extremely famous and have a well-documented love of great literature.

"What I want, Charles, is to be considered one of the great salonists of our time, perhaps of all time. I want my salon to be greater than the one Stein and Toklas hosted in gay Paree a full century ago, a salon as yet unsurpassed in terms of glamour and intellectual muscle, the one commentators never mention without adding the word 'legendary'. I want my salon to be not just legendary but *more legendary than theirs*. I want, above all, to go down in history as the legendary Lupin McTaggart. Surely," she cried, "surely that's not too much to ask!"

Growing Dumb: An Autobiography of an English Education
by Peter Quartermain

(Zat-So Productions, Montréal – Vancouver, 2021)

Ian Brinton

In his Preface to this unforgettable memoir Peter Quartermain brings us immediately face-to-face with the power of language:

> To 'utter', a word I love, comes from deep in the throat. It comes from a void. We don't know what we are doing when we come to utterance. Closer to stutter than to mutter, both of which contain it. To utter is to bring language to the edge of the sayable.

As he reconstructs his childhood recollections of what happened to himself and his family in September 1939, the day war broke out, he presents us with the exactness of what one would later come to expect from a man who wrote so sensitively and precisely about the Objectivists in America and about Basil Bunting in the North of England. The actual day war broke out is vividly there in the 'dust hanging in the air from the coconut matting all rolled up one side of the kitchen' and 'it was the slow drip of the kitchen tap I could hardly reach.' The importance of what we come to recognise as 'home', whether this was in the Birmingham of the British Midlands or in country villages brings to mind what Gaston Bachelard wrote about the poetics of space when he suggested that 'by approaching the house images with care not to break up the solidarity of memory and imagination, we may hope to make others feel all the psychological elasticity of an image that moves us at an unimaginable depth.'

As the Quartermain family moved to the village of Wheaton Aston it was to a place that was never to feel like home:

> …home was in Shirley, lots of houses, lots of shops, lots of buses and cars and the baker's boy and the milkman delivering stuff every morning and a set of traffic lights and a public park with lots of flower beds and a playground with lots of swings and a sandbox.

The repetitions here emphasise the actuality of what was being lost by the move and it is appropriate perhaps to call to mind the comments made by Quartermain in his publication for the Basil Bunting Archive in Durham in 1990:

> Language. Language divorced from the immediate is language divorced from what he [Bunting] called "our deepest nature".
>
> (*Basil Bunting: Poet of the North*)

Quartermain also recalled for us that Basil Bunting had admired the sixteenth-century French poet Malherbe because whenever he had written anything he would go down to the market in Caen and ask the women there to read it to him and he would then pay them if there were any words they didn't know:

> He didn't expect them to understand what he was aiming at or even enjoy the poem, but he wished above all things to be meticulous about keeping his language clear and plain.

It is no wonder that Francis Ponge was such an admirer of Malherbe nor is it any surprise that Peter Quartermain should be such an admirer of the Objectivist world of poetry as represented by George Oppen and Louis Zukofsky, Carl Rakosi and Charles Reznikoff, Lorine Niedecker and Basil Bunting. In order to be able to communicate the sharp sense of 'thereness', the reality of the past brought to the immediacy of the present, you have to *'learn* to see things the way other people do.' Quartermain's prose presents us with that vivid reality of a past which still haunts a present and one is struck by the way in which an opening, *une ouverture* as Philippe Jaccottet would have put it, reveals a world that seems immediately alive:

> You'd open the cowshed door, pushing through bits of heavy sacking to keep the light from shining out, they smelled of jute and grain and seed, and you'd suddenly be in a different world, the smell of cows, the steady rhythm of milk hissing tinnily into pails, the note shifting as the milk rose higher, straw on the floor and a cow pissing into the gutter behind it, black ropy spiderwebs up in the rafters…

In addition to the wealth of family memories brought to life in this autobiography there are whole sections which deal with the nature of schooling and the strange world of the boarding community with its own rules and pathways that have to be followed. One is often reminded of Dickens's Dotheboys Hall as the Headmaster 'called us all in to The Big Room' to shout at us that "The forecourt is out-of-bounds! When you come into this building you use the back or the side door":

> Nobody had ever spoken to me like that before, he was the most terrifying man I'd ever met…

The world of the 1940s boarding-school in a rural British setting is brought to life in such a way that you can *feel* the emptiness of the School on a Sunday 'so palpable you could almost touch it, the silence so strong you could *hear* it':

> Matron nowhere to be found, the Housemaster nowhere to be found, the kitchen closed down, tables and counters clean, all the dishes on their shelves, the clock quietly ticking, everything in its proper place, no one round the bike sheds, all of us left to fend for ourselves…

However, there is another side to schooling and it is both sharp perception and a widening literary perspective that permits Quartermain to associate his own milking of cows on the farm with the experience of childhood familiarity portrayed by D.H. Lawrence in *The Rainbow* which he went on to read in the early 1950s recognising a 'familiar chord':

> Even now as I write this I can feel the warmth radiating from that complete otherness of the cow, that flow of quiet energy profoundly indifferent to my own, the sheer uncompromising physicality obscurely disturbing no matter how familiar as I chivvied cows about in the fields or when I milked one, the idea of it, that mild oiliness building up on my skin as I pulled on those teats, it sticks between my fingers near the knuckle joints as I sit and think on it…

Memories leave their relics on the beach and as Rachel Blau DuPlessis points out in her words which close this remarkable volume the prose rhythms of Peter Quartermain's sentences leave 'a whole bunch of sea wrack, shells and old plastic on our shore'. This is a book that must be read.

Three Poems

Kat Peddie

Blue Boy

*An alternative interpretative text to the painting by Thomas
Gainsborough*

Don't wanna do what the old masters tell me no
Don't wanna be background no
backup dancer me I

am centre stage
in my shining shining powder blue with the poise of an
Absolutely fucking fantastic artist

        Everything else is just mud

I leave it all behind me.

Hey, Joshy, mate, here I am a little boy blue sneering at all
your fucking sky,
not a little lost boy am a big boy I

can blow my own trumpet thank you
who needs *chiaroscuro* when you have braggadocio

Offspring of a cock fight

don't have blue balls

I am not a sad boy am a swaggering boy
Repeat after me
Like the cut of my
Blue satin romper

You can get away with anything with the right attitude &
the right attitude is to know
you can get away with anything

I don't play by the rules yeah
these red flags I am waving, look how sexy they are
& you know you want a piece of me don't you
yes

Chatterton

(alternative interpretative texts to the painting by Henry Wallis)

I.　　I gave my lover genital warts

It is tempting to say
I really am so very sorry. It really is nothing to be ashamed of they say
it is very ordinary, one out of a hundred of you have it
right now

If you believe half of what they say, back then 9 out of 10 artists had syphilis
and all of them were men. There are fields where
a history of constant innovation can be called progress.

It is tempting to say   I really just couldn't help it
It is just so sexy being a forger, the way you get
to be an 'exceedingly studious child' & fussy fussy
on the detail & still a bit of a rogue.

It is hard holding this thing called personality together
It is tempting to say   I feel terrible
                                             to be so careless with your life
when you live among others is not really good enough. I used
to be the picture, the very poster boy,
of youth. I have been posing as Chatterton.

It is tempting to throw yourself down in an attitude of swooning at how
our pleasures are so connected with our pain &
how I am so very alone now & feel so very near
dying.

II.   **Chatterton**

What is important is the red hair
           like Christ, like all the beautiful women have
What is important is the red hair and the blue trews
it is just such a lovely blue, and with that red held just apart it is just   yes
What is important is the framing
What is important is the moment of dying,   how very
young he is
What is important is the attitude of the poet
What is important is the choices he made
how he very slowly throws his arm out   a gesture   yes   like this

Van Gogh on the banks of the Seine

Here you can see Van Gogh absorb the lessons of pointillism

Sometimes it goes dot to dot to dot to dot &
Here I am

Here Van Gogh is almost at the point of grand narrative
                almost at the point of becoming a great artist

Here you can take respite and relief from city life through nature

Here you can take respite from the darkness you can see it in the
    colours and the brushstroke the

Swish swish

Joy joy

Flower flower grass stem paint the

Dot dot dot &
Dash dash   -

            Pointillism: that we are all made of
            cells & smeared boundaries

you go dot to dot to dot and the idea is that something greater emerges

Here it is the Seine

Here it is the suffering artist in his brief discovery of joy. It is yellow like

Isn't it always
the Pont du Clichy is blues and yellows and green. Say
                            I might be happy if I go to Paris
                            I might be happy if I get out of Paris
                            Might be happy if I get more plein air

Might paint a picture almost entirely of yellow

Clichy on the tv is mostly greyscale   The cops will raid a mobile
phone shop looking for children, for drugs. They will save the
children, mostly, from traffickers, turn them
over to the state.

There is an element of justice.   Before he went to Paris
to dull colours, Van Gogh often added black to his paint

This is how we can tell it is realism.

In the months before spring
I stuck something smaller than my elbow in my ear so far I can still
    hear the ringing

Not 'in a rage' exactly but trying to displace something that was
    causing pain

I cannot absorb all the lessons of the old masters
                        take endless self-portraits at significant
                        points of my life

it takes time to absorb the new the really new thing
it is not always new like spring is new, arriving in the same form of
    newness in regular time
though spring does not really do that   it goes dot to dot to dot &
something that we might be able to make shape with emerges &
sometimes there is too much wax in the ear for all the oil there is to
    ever draw out the blockage &

yes the thing that surprises is often joy, arriving with its flurried
excitements & its not knowing and maybe imagining a shape
bringing in its new disappointments &
yes
there is a person behind the painting in the painting
            Maybe it looks   or
is at the point of jumping into the landscape &
really it is very small

Prose Poems

John Olson

Whenever I Feel The Spirit

Whenever I feel the spirit I like to dance myself into a frenzy of luminous bacteria. Who doesn't love ambiguity? It's why I read Frank O'Hara and lost control of my phobias a long time ago. Most people don't like helicopters in their hair. So why would they like poetry? I like having big thoughts and strange appetites. I carry a sack of ink whenever I go and marvel at the stubbornness of ears. The narratives that embroider our perceptions are backyards of splintered wood and dirt, damp basements with raggedy old couches and linoleum ghosts. Symmetry is the milk of bondage. The hills explain everything. And just as I began to understand my shirt, I found the strange red light of a hornet in a paper bag, and it made me feel imminent and involved, like the creaking wood floors of used bookstores, when they existed, a long time ago, in the Age of Books, and Tarzan and pterodactyls wed in a lingua franca of lush incongruities.

Electric Cables On A Rainy Night

That night in Seattle 1975 before I'd shaken California off and I was living in a studio apartment with a stone fireplace and a big kitchen and the bus line was right out my window buses with electric cables that made a sparkly sound especially on rainy nights water beaded in the window lit up by a streetlight and 10cc came on the radio by my mattress & sang "I'm Not In Love" & it gave me a strong feeling I won't say romantic not exactly there's something beautifully sad & ambivalent in the song more like that interval of time when you're still alone and desires run loose in all directions and nothing could happen and everything could happen in a split second. The air seems preternaturally rich. The room is quiet but there's a palpable stirring, an indefinable presence, a subtle agitation of potential energy measurable in joules. Imagine all the images sleeping in the language waiting to be awakened. A fever rumbles in the words at the far margin of our existence. There's wine in the air, & power. Electric cables on a rainy night.

Word Spurt

There are words I don't know. I would tell you what they are, but I don't know. What words, precisely, I just can't say. I just know that one day, one moment, one tiny tear in the fabric of time, and I will experience something and then try to find a word, or words, for that thing. But what if the only words I can find to best describe an experience – a smell, a texture, a sprain – are in another language? What if it lies in a sprawl of words, too obscured by words, to be wit- nessed as anything other than a brawl, a sticky cocoon, when it pops out of the air? When it crawls across the floor. When it sits down and lights a cigar. When it voyages to the right of you, smiling as it goes by, on its quest for experience, and the sheer joy of moving around in space, which all words love to do, they love to get out there and reveal things, invent things, phrase things, freeze things, matriculate ejaculate and spurt things. Do you see what I mean? Do you know what words I'm talking about? I don't even know what words I'm talking about.

Breath Of The Morning

I feel the edge of the world in the breath of the morning. The dizzying liquor of possibility. That moment when everything is so clearly delineated it could never be a song. It could only be a weekday, a frontier with a schedule in it. It's hard for me to say this but the truth of marble isn't in its density but the nobility of its influence, how it affects the hands when you're leaning on it to gaze at yourself in the mirror wondering who the person might be behind that face in the glass. Images are the shadows of a brighter reality. The fire is behind us. The hotel is just a rationalization. Everything is an instance of poetry. But not everybody sees it. Kiowa hunt buffalo. It's 1854. Arthur Rimbaud has just been born. Franz Liszt's *Orpheus* premieres. A philosophy walks out of the sun and splashes down somewhere near Omaha, which has just been established as a trading post. Essences are axles. But it's the wheels that make things roll.

This

I like this. This this. This morsel of grammar. This demonstrative adjective. This implicative this. This fist of this. This bucket of this. Those sounds buckets make when they're full of impertinence. This reliquary of irrelevance. This butte. This mine of crystal. This Bristol epistle. This bristle. This whistle. This vision on the verge of epiphany. This moment in time. This germination of manners in a meat locker of the mind. But no. This isn't it. Not it at all. This is.

What Is A Word

What is a word, Nietzsche asks. The image of a nerve stimulus in sound, he answers. I think it's a small lacquered netsuke. Nougat. Nugget. Cordial cherries. 10 pieces. Net Wt. 6.6 oz. Artificially flavored. Classic good taste. Dark chocolate. Lift to indulge, it says on the box. Real cherries. May contain pits or pit fragments. Viking remains. Helmet and sword. The bones of a dog. The wings of a dragon. But to infer from the nerve stimulus, Nietzsche continues, a cause outside us, that is already the result of a false and unjustified application of the principle of reason. But why bring reason in? We should leave it outside to soak in the rain.

Beeswax

Consciousness is essentially beeswax. It might also be the meaning inside this sentence buzzing around a fragrant ambiguity. Well-being is essentially plumage. It's ok to whistle if you can feel it in the shoulder, like a twinge of socialism, or a wing. Sometimes the grazing of animals reminds me of feet. This has been proven many times by the sensuality of language rubbed on a flight attendant. Sometimes a simple frequency can do quick little jerks & create an ambience of fluoro-scopes & ottoman while the fog bends itself into a heart & strawberries cause stucco. There are regions of the mind that submerge you in uncertainty when they're done bruising you with awareness. They leave you in a trance, dripping & unrecognizable. This is how I learn. I crack an egg & look at the contents spread into geese. Why is reality so big & incoherent? Think of a house. If you want to find me, I'll be in the narrative next door letting words happen to me.

I Need A Way

I need a way to make my indiscretions more palatable. Clearly there is an experience called 'irrelevant.' There is an energy in the head demanding conversations with the world. The essential thing is to carve a pumpkin and fill it with words. Words like doing things. West African rivers are coalitions of wine and informality. There are chemicals involved in the vocabulary of space. Thoughts weigh nothing. But be careful. Life is hard. You're going to require energy and whistles, scabbards and magnetism. Meaning feeds the mind thousands of variables. You can hear the sand boil in Arizona. Spinoza saw God as nature itself. And why not? Mania defines the moment. It gets all over everything. Propellers churn the emotions into sugar and that's what people do. They pour drinks & talk about the future, which is embryonic and glittery, vivid as a vocal cord stuck in a closet all day, waiting for someone to say something.

Three Poems

Nancy Gaffield

«Variations on a theme»

Blue
returns as
     imagined. No kelp forests here in
     this blue vitrine I am
        inundated while you
watch,
your tongue stuck
     on ice. Once a possibility like
     waves frozen in motion
        now less oxygen and more
heat
and acid
     a solitary ice floe, loose white
     crystals, translucent bluish layers.
        I am an outlier
shuck-
ling in melt.
     Is it possible to think into

the future? Runways underwater
    ghosts of planes submerged
in
duck-egg blue
    all the ash filtered out like the flashes
    of colour you saw in the detritus
       of the Grindelwald
ice
once sent to
    Paris for fashionable cocktails but
    the glaciers declined. The Arctic is
       unravelling, roads buckle
the
house is
    sinking. How blue is my canvas
    layered with broken glass and scattered
       light, the point of brink.
Blue
a single
    syllable blown into the air, morning-
    glory blue, orgone energy blue, gestures from
       the dolour of deep ice.

(«Variations on a theme» *is subtitled 'Splintered Ice No. 2', painted
by the Cornish artist Wilhelmina Barns-Graham. By forging different
phenomena into a kind of unity, the poem seeks to create the same
kind of unity as the painting through patterning. The form is thus a key
element here.*)

«Heiliger Dankgesang»

when no cure exists
there are notes
        and poems
for the slow drawing down
just these

notes and words   in a minor key
            charms

                                    earth-noise   earth-rooted
                                                         threnody
                                              implace me where
                                        the cello's seductive syntax
                                             bends like a sentence
                                        the simple trick of dissonance
                                                    up an octave
                                                         until
                                              thin strands of glass
                                                         quiver

today's freezing rain thrums
in a key I cannot hear
sets my heart to breaking
        strip it down
eight notes become five
five become three
        now reduce it to two
        one
        [ ]

                            exhalation of ancient yews in the Lydian mode
                                              life breathes down
                                                 to the point of
                                                    dissolve
                                              still I persevere
                                              can't let it go

when the flower blooms   the sepal opens
forsythia corresponds
                    ambiguity
                    soft to the core
separate the cellulose from the wood
        work with the pulp of
trills | syncopations | harmonies
        against

                the immense
            terrible   silence
conflicting currents
meet in the vortex
            the roundness of sound
                    spinning
                            slow | fast | slow | fast | slow
beyond the range of illness
beyond the yawning tombstones
                    their names buffered
                    by time and lichen

                                            it's harder to live
                                         as twilight scythes
                                 a snow-covered landscape
                                        walled up in winter
                                     the notes reduce from
                                                    f to *e*
                                            e comes on

suppose you could step out into the night sky
fly stowaway with the Perseids
            bathe the hemispheres
            with stardust
the notes sustain
                    how we swam
                    in their saline chords

(«*Heiliger Dankgesang*» or '*Holy Song of Thanksgiving*' is
Beethoven's third movement of Opus 132 String Quartet, written
when he was recovering from a near fatal illness. The poem attempts
to borrow aspects of Beethoven's compositional procedure.)

«*Lepanto*»

bawling fleet flock   cruel lottery   horned minotaur
fair hair / breast   the spine

trembles
unravelled grief

Apollo pulls back the spurs
the frenzy
stops

deep gloom-grove
Stygian marsh   Styx playing a tune
they flit   through
lightning
where gold shone   a glittering twig
wash it
anoint it

[wailing

raise the body
torch it   blood in bowls
to smote
a lamb
entrails on flames

BASTARDS
hubbub wanders the riverbank
no pilot to steer the tiller   I swam the place of shadows
[Dido

wandering
crying   O
pen

wound
our awful horse fucked

O blessed grove
snakes / gates / maws

girdled groan

some happy shades picnicking
for mother and country
the field hums
drunk   on forgetfulness
the sea's marbled surface
stuff hardens   a mound / a crowd

~~memory~~ erased
twin plumes of doubt   down at the mouth ships
                                        stand to shore

(«Lepanto» *is the title of a painting cycle by Cy Twombly depicting
the 16th century sea battle led by the papal states against the
Ottoman invasion. This poem responds to that subject by taking
the text of Virgil's Aeneid, Book VI 'The Visit to Hell' (transl. David
Hadbawnik). The poem is a work of erasure and of translation in the
sense of carrying across, from one language to another, one culture to
another, one time and place to another.)*

Seven Poems

Ralph Hawkins

Yeast

how would you know I was still here, pacing up and down

what am I wearing tonight, taffeta

rich daisy dress of meadow sweet, a cherry

waiting in the dock yard with trays of canapés

for the sailors returning from the war

the hotel busy with the laundry delivery,

white camomile with lilac sprays

a headdress from the Indies, a girl from Clapham,

but you, I deranged of honeycomb and sweetmeats

my lines, my tender touch, these days of late late sunshine

O you, between the aspen and the holm, the river

first seeds and then flowers pass near water meadows

if an image is static is it lodged in time

door after door in the hallway

acquisition

everything lately seems to be extraordinary
zucchini in flagrant flower
an unnatural dehiscence

the damask plum hoicked
from the child's bowl
filled with inflated hope

and there at the simmering horizon
sailors tuck into turtled soup, octopus
or a gob full of oysters

his daughter banging a toy drum
up and down the Victorian promenade,
Empress of India

24 hour traffic

24 hour traffic along the Tokyo Port Seaside Road

Mr Haruo Wako drives his empty Isuzu freezer truck back to the depot

such small wonder the baby boy is well fed and chubby

the circulation of commodities such as high-end art or

the lifestyles of celebrities,

whose opinions seem to matter no end

but don't impinge on Mrs Wako who works as an office cleaner

whilst her mother looks after the two children

once a supporter of the Japanese Red Army

the heuristics of being egg-bound (liquid paraffin)

the plant room in the factory (where no plant had presence) the day begins
where on earth could we go, progressing economies driving us on from the wooden plough

high as red kites in love over our heads not wanting to come back down to earth
a number of labour camps, cramped workshops, and forest fires, too late to ask for a refund

we settle for a hayrick with a peasant, at least the weather seemed good
a few sweet mice, mallows and a patch of free-floating algae from the sewage farm

look, said Maisy, there are creatures you've never dreamed of
was she overstepping the mark reading about surplus value in das capital

and when the machines started up and the winding wheel you couldn't hear yourself breathe

by the age of five I was reading vita nuova, mummy holding my small hand guiding me around
Florence, was it there we saw the faces of angels angled towards heaven, faces of pale blancmange

with their fat baby feet – is that what they did for a living, how they got by
was it possible to recognise your child in that divine longevity

at that time there were a lot of loose men roaming around Europe dabbling in
crime and philandry, some with bright curls and large organs pumping out

tunes in grand settings, a blind beggar and a leper walking over the Tuscan hills, mackerel clouds above,

short shift, all that grease and oil, a way of life that only the poor and maimed could survive,
real poets, consumptive, arms dealers, vagabonds standing at the bar spouting nonsense

from a chair in the garden, reading

a cross-bill comes down to the pool to drink

finding ourselves in an unfamiliar place

an outhouse of plants to tender

the flare of an evening's sky close to a metalled road

sparks of orange and tangerine

he is walking again

the song of the wren lifting the ornamental grass

not long now

some trees will survive, reaching out

birds lovingly tangled in their branches

root memory of esso gas pumps, oil and shale

the local food store with its doorbell

the call of a green finch on his iPhone

pom-poms

I can hear the turbines turn over in the engine room,

the water kept at a steady flow

with bourgeoise bustles, top hats and canes

and of course there are dogs done up like dinners

all is contingent

the summer park full of children

a chocolate sponge, a raised pie and a flan of some description

birds in willow trees chat about their life-spans

and which seeds and insects they prefer

plucked from the nest they fit right in to nature's plan

(somewhat on hold or not?)

Raoul thinks about writing a pom-pom poem for his teacher

full of pom-poms and roses and old cupboards

the air astringent from the sewage overspills

right now his sister, soon to be a marine biologist,

wants to feed the ravenous ducks

a fat man releases a bulldog

a cornerstone of leisure

looking closely at Seurat's la grande jatte

there are similarities to *our* world

the future belching and full of waste

and yet still dreaming of the preconditional

my changing moods

the sky has its reign of blue
hence its wow factor
which guides us away at times
from thoughts of pain, disease
and drudgery. Mosaics capture
little of the fine detail of the shade
and the cool of the Mesquite,
a seashell sound of whispers
in a cloister, a sadness descends
like a milky eye, no longer
watchful, recalling his lover's
kiss (that wow factor) his mouth
opening in astonishment
making a life out of writing
down her dreams, that *tsk tsk*
you read in a poem, that milky eyed
cloud cover covering over
the over manicured lawns
awaiting their midnight guests
gaining weight as they go
gastropod after gastropod
eating their way through life

until they reach that crossing-point
turnips in a open field
"not as many peanuts these days"
said Maisy, she'll be ten next
birthday and then there is a path
with a woman walking with a
pom-pomeranian

from *Now, Here, This: Half-Sonnets*

Ron Silliman

for Terence Winch & Ivan Sokolov

I

Look. Tinnitus whistles somewhere behind me. Three crows on the lawn.

Numb thumb.

Beyond the forest preserve, 202 offers its soft white noise. Deadheading the camellias, sharing pink petals with fat bees confused by the climate. The new guy two doors up.

Amahl and the Light Sabers. Mr Iguana to top it off. Leave leaves on the lawn. Are you allowed to do that?

Geese in Bulgaria. Early morning ear worm, some Dylan tune I'd never learned the words to. Cementitious.

The unlikely thrush. The keyboard cold at dawn. Point in the dream where I begin to ask questions, like why is it always Kit? A heavier fork. One red light blinking through the forest.

A multiple theremin, being a large triangular shaped box roughly the size of a grand piano with multiple antennae or dealie-bobs sticking up played by up to three musicians at a time to the right of the stage alongside the rest of the ensemble which does in fact include, at the far left, a grand piano.

II

I awaken, soaking wet. The snow is not melting. A filament of hydrogen, 3,900 light years long. Count to four.

Vowels, parts per million. Three els, two peas. Then that was a third. The shooting got worse right at sunrise. With its Stay-Back program, the CIA, as the OSS was now called, created mercenary teams, armies actually, in every nation in Europe. Olof Palme's last motion picture was Kurosawa's Ran. Olson, contemplating putting moves on Elizabeth Bishop.

All those stone steps. Exit through the barber shop.

Each period a tourniquet in the flow of words. In winter, you see neighbors' houses light up at five in the morning, the screen of trees stripped bare. The heaviest of three hoodies. We've been here before.

The lid to the compost bucket heavy with ice. History bleaches: blood runs into the sewer but then it's gone. Kids love to roll down a hill but a somersault is a skill. I stare at the mistyped word. Word vs. wood, wch one?

Small bananas. Cell phone in the "wrong" pocket. Concept of a day, a year, of 30 years. A notion of "wrong," song.

Leaf-blowers in the woods. Venona, come closer, touch softly. Half sonnet. My flurona. The September pogrom in the Pera district of Istanbul. The Tulsa poets never wrote once of Greenwood. Tom

Cromwell watching while Tyndale gets lit up. A coup in Wilmington. Unlike, say, thieves or traitors "necklaced" with flaming tires in South Africa, gesticulating wildly, vainly attempting to free themselves of the flames, the Buddhist monks of Vietnam sit zazen, utterly still as they surrender in smoke.

III

Museums matter, but how they raise funds to operate matters even more. There is no past tense. First beep of a fire alarm jolts me awake, but the room, though dark, is silent.

Such suck. The south side of the house is filled with light, but out a north window I still see patches of snow. My hand lightly on your hip. Winter canopy alive with birds. My great-great grandfather still signed his name with an X.

The furnace has begun to growl. You snore, just a little, snore and twitch. Artificial tears. I had not contemplated the water in the basement.

My pod, quite odd. The tips of my thumbs bloody with winter. That moment near dawn when the canopy of the forest is almost golden with light, the houses below still shrouded by night. Sentence, sentence, sentence.

Oke as in joke. Bök. Awkward in the outback. Purple is a purple word.

Now, here, this. My mother's bravery at the age of 22. Cracks across the tips of my thumbs. The impact of two degrees on the cost of petrol over the whole of the house. A volcano on Hunga-Tunga.

Light before sun. The white oaks die, one after another, transforming the canopy even in winter. The new neighbor across the street likes to leave her garage door open. So-called white noise of the distant freeway drowned by the furnace one flight below. When this you see, make a cup of tea.

excerpt from *Mice 1961*

Stacey Levine

(This novel takes place in 1961, at a party in Miami.)

I heard a huge commotion. Down the hallway, off in a small, crowded splinter-hall leading to the bathroom, the party's host Bianchi called, his voice large and resonant: "Marge! Get that monster out a' the tub!"

I drifted toward the crowd, peering through gaps between neighbors' long bodies and the apertures of bent elbows, squeezing into the splinter-hall.

The small bathroom was mobbed with high-spirited guests. Angling stiffly as an outsized penny through the crowd, I managed to get in and soon lodged myself between the sink and a damp hamper.

"Aw but Sal. He's cute!" It was Eddleston.

I caught sight of the claw-footed bathtub.

Then the city's head librarian Florence Stroke called from the hallway, voice strong above the others', "What's everybody looking at?" and tried squeezing into the bathroom as well, but the pack of neighbors in the door area did not open or budge. So the woman remained in the hallway holding her purse in one hand, slightly left-out looking, unable to see the bathtub with its few inches of water where a baby alligator clambered.

Marge had somehow gotten into the bathroom, however, her hip pushed against the sink, which was filled with soapwater and combs. "In the tub? Oh that's just *Khrushchev*," she told everyone, gesturing loosely, as if to make the creature seem more part of things.

Another librarian, Millie, had shoved herself into the crowd and now seemed smaller than she really was. "Oh the darling!" she said, looking at the tub, tender.

Eddleston explained to them all, "Yeah! I got this lil 'gator for seventy cents at the Pet Ranch in Allapattah. He was a present for Sheila."

"I'm a cheap date," Sheila admitted, grinning.

"Allapattah? Why that area's all Spanish now," side-remarked Moose Riley, a local surfer, newly arrived to the party, holding a small box under one arm and grasping his surfboard in the other.

"The Spanish moved there? Oh that's too bad," said Cissy.

Millie then stumbled against a towel-holder, causing the crowd to sway en masse. "But it's always that way Moose," she told the surfer. "Neighborhoods always change—and for the worse. They used to have big lunches at Spatt's but no more. It was torn down. And now *Allapattah's* changing? Why does everything go downhill?"

"Now wait," said the local clerk Minnie in her delicate voice, grasping a neighbor's shoulder for balance, "Aren't changes usually for the better?"

"Could be. Potato chips changed the snack world," asserted Moates from the crowd.

Some in the bathroom nodded seriously, seeming to agree.

"Larry! Are potatoes people?" It was Millie, annoyed at the illogic of it.

Then Bianchi called to them from the hallway: "Hey. First of all th'Spanish can come into my business any time. But that Khrushchev?" He jerked his thumb. "Get him out."

Neighbors laughed; the little bathroom seemed to vibrate.

Marge called over to Bianchi, her fiancé. "Aw Sal! Let Khruschchev swim in the tub awhile! He likes it."

The baker shifted uncertainly. "But what if somebody needs the toilet?"

"Let him stay," Eddleston urged the party's host. "A 'gator could grow on you Sal. Cute isn't he—Khrushchev? He eats grapes."

Moates slipped through the crowd, holding a square tumbler, saying eagerly, "Let *me* see this thing." Pale juice sloshed, wetting his fingers. "Ah look at funny little Khrushchev! Lotsa energy he has."

The alligator chafed his lime-green feet quickly against the tub wall.

Laughter rushed around the bathroom again. Soon the creature's lemonade-yellow eyes rested just above the water's surface, his elastic sides pulling in and out with his breath.

Who could see what he saw?

A voice strained in distantly from the hallway—it was The Woman Who Didn't Speak. "I agree with Mr. Bianchi! Why should a reptile be in the bathroom? It's unappetizing I tell you."

"Oh *her*," whispered Cissy from the thick of the crowd, and Florence shushed her.

Then the crowd shuffled as one, for Remnick came through, pulling his sleepy-looking daugher by the hand. He stooped beside the tub. "There's the little 'gator. See?" he told Phyllis gently. "They don't live long like we do."

The child gazed at the reptile, her hand on the tub wall. She looked just like her mother. But neighbors seemed to love Phyllis more than they did Nina.

"I said is anyone going to remove that animal?" repeated The Woman Who Didn't Speak. Before that evening, I'd never heard her talk, for generally she communicated via rough, quick hand-gestures.

The Woman stepped into the bathroom easily; everyone parted the way for her. In moments she stood near me by the hamper, the small bucket-like purse still on her forearm, expensive looking: calf.

From the center of the pack of guests came a small, melty voice: It was Honey. "Ooh just look at Khrushchev's little face. What a doll!"

"Yer nuts!" said the surfer Riley. "That lizard'd murder you for lunch first thing he gets hungry."

"Keep your fingers away everyone," Florence warned them. "It's an *animal*. Don't forget that. An animal with big teeth."

Then The Woman, weary looking, leaning on the papery hamper, repeated with irritation: "*Please*. Quit yakking and remove that lizard. That thing belongs in the Serpen*tarium*."

"All right ma'am," said Eddleston, stepping toward the tub and holding a towel, as if ready to trap the alligator. Yet suddenly he stopped and seemed to drop the idea altogether, turning to Moates, nudging the man. "Hey Larry. Betcha fifty cents this lizard'll be dead in a week."

The importer's eyes crinkled. "Why not? Maybe I could make a few coins."

Eyes slitted, the alligator appeared to doze atop the water.

Moates joked: "And by the way where's this monster's wife? Where's Mrs. Alligator?"

"Alligators don't have wives," said little Phyllis flatly from beside the bathtub, and the adults' laughter filled the bathroom again.

Laughing Moates pointed at the child, telling the others, "She's onta something! Hey. You people wanna know why Khruschchev's got no lizard girlfriend? 'Cause he's a conniving SOB!"

Neighbors laughed yet again, though this time less vigorously. The Woman Who Didn't Speak gazed at the tubwater in disgust, though with a salty-type humor on the one hand and pent-up intensity as well, she burst out, "For the last time will somebody do as Mr. Bianchi said and get that miserable creature outside? This is a *party*. Not a *barn*. And I tell you that lizard's a *sonofabitch with scales*."

At this, silence fell over the bathroom. Marge and Sheila exchanged glances.

"Oh I know. You'll talk about me later won't you? When I'm out of earshot," The Woman said, then laughed once, hard, without smiling, in a gust.

"Please don't think that," Marge told her. "We wouldn't discuss you."

The Woman Who Didn't Speak kept her eyes on the young alligator. "Why would I believe you? And as for this animal—look at its nose. Tell me how could God make such a yoogly chump? When somebody's really ugly I call him 'yoo-gly.' Doesn't that word make him even uglier?" The Woman stared at Sheila, who looked to her fiance.

"C'mon Burt. Let's take Kruschchev outside," she called, and Eddleston returned with the towel.

"*Finally,*" The Woman said tersely, leaning on the hamper, setting up to watch the capture, a harsh scent on her breath that reminded me of loss and dust.

Eddleston bent to the tub. "All right—I'll get him now."

"Just take him 'round the neck Burt," urged the surfer.

The alligator's curved mouth in the water appeared to smile.

"Look! Khrushchev knows we're talking about him!" cried Phyllis. "Daddy I love Khrushchev."

"Listen little girl," The Woman Who Didn't Speak told the alarmed-looking child. "Do you see the sonafabitch's teeth? They'll grow as he grows. They'll turn green."

"Ma'am please," said Remnick. "Don't speak to Phyllis like that." He held the child's shoulder with his palm.

Then Eddleston ducked in quickly, snatching the alligator into the towel. As Khrushchev struggled, the man stumbled into the crowd, squeezing the animal's head or neck—it was too much force. Then he stood still.

The room went silent, neighbors' mouths flat and straight.

I heard someone gasp, and Florence stepped close to the towel, saying, "Oh Poor Khrushchev! He was just a *baby,*" with a wobbling softness in her throat: Her heart.

Andrea Brady, *The Blue Split Compartments*

(Wesleyan University Press, 2021)

Ian Brinton

Publishing poetry is a very public matter involving certain formal rules and practices and, as an early review of Andrea Brady's 2006 critical examination of the *English Funerary Elegy in the Seventeenth Century* makes clear, the poem, 'like the rituals of deathbed, lying in the coffin, procession, sermon and interment, was part of the process by which the transition between life and death was publicly marked, and the communal solidarity of the bereaved re-affirmed as the dead person was progressively distanced from the living.' (Paul Dean, *The Use of English*, Vol. 58, Number 2). On the back cover of Brady's recently published deeply moving sequence of lyric poems exploring the relationships between military drone operators and their victims Laleh Khalili alerts the reader to that sense of powerful formality:

> Word by affecting word, image by terrifying image, these powerfully harrowing poems tell the story of modern imperial warfare, hellish technologies of death, and unacknowledged faraway victims.

When *The Blue Split Compartments* was published in June last year it was accompanied by a Press Release which highlighted some of the background to the creation of the poems:

> Drawing on chatroom logs, military policy manuals, pattern of life archives, and accounts by witnesses around the world, these poems document the consequences of the perpetual and 'everywhere war' conducted from remote airbases, where pilots in shipping containers surveil and destroy remote 'objects'.

The last section of Andrea Brady's box of poems is devoted to notes on the text in which she describes the sequence as a suite of poems for the drone age:

> It inhabits a variety of compartments: the remote split operations in which control of the drone is transferred from local crews to pilots in shipping containers in the Nevada desert; the compartmentalized or split psyches which allow soldiers to commute to war from the suburbs; the colony as what Franz Fanon called a 'world divided into compartments,' its zones for settler and 'native' occupation strictly policed; the patrolled blue skies which victims fear more than cloud; blue-on-blue friendly fire; and the tactical innovation known as 'kill boxes'.

As we read these poems we become increasingly aware that whole areas of the earth have been transformed into 'open air prisons' and I am reminded of what Michel Foucault wrote about Panopticism when he suggested that the major effect of Jeremy Bentham's invention had been to induce in the prison inmate a state of conscious and permanent visibility that assures the automatic functioning of power. Brady's poems make us aware of the constant buzzing of drones overhead which induce 'profound trauma and changes to social life':

> The victim can hear but not see the drone. The drone pilot can see but not hear their victim. What is the meaning of this relation?

Andrea Brady's close awareness of both the power and the limitations of language has been a measure of her poetry for many years and whilst reading the poems in *The Blue Split Compartments* I felt steered back to remind myself of 'Sung to Sleep' from the 2013 Reality Street volume *Cut from the Rushes*:

> What viewer could believe them
> that a locum spirit floats life through it,
> connecting all in death and harmony,
> that there is a god for forces: in spring
> a diverse country
> blots moving randomly in vacuums
> everywhere full of water, and so full of life.

In one of the 'Activated' poems from this current sequence we are presented with an uncompromising statement from a box:

> Naming specifies the object, draws it
>   apart from the brute
> materiality, grounds it in relation to all others.

Name becomes annihilation, 'expelling / the person from the vacuum' and this voice says with a tone of incontrovertible correctness

> We bring specificity to an end,
>   dispersing gravel and carbon granules
>   over the open field
>   where we run the prey.

In that early book on 'Funerary Elegy' Brady had quoted the seventeenth-century poet Ralph Knevet's lines

> Griefe is a passion, and all passions must
> Confined be, unto a measure just.

She went on to add that 'Like music, prosody draws on the divine order of the cosmos' and that like the rites of mourning themselves it is a matter of 'keeping time'. The convincing range of lyric voices in this new sequence is measured and whilst the concerns which lie behind so many of the poems are both political and angry there is never a moment which prevents them from being deeply bound up with the haunting quality of grief, that which informs the passing of time and may come out of the blue.

Three Poets in New York: Charles Bernstein and Pierre Joris with Habib Tengour

(published in *El Watan* (Algeria), December 5, 2021)

Habib Tengour: *Dear Charles, dear Pierre, it is a pleasure to find myself in New York, more exactly in Brooklyn, where you both live. Thank you, Charles, for inviting us to your place for lunch. I am now living in Iowa as part of the International Writing Program and taking advantage of my brief New York visit to ask you some questions (it was a friend from Mostaganem who requested I interview New York poets for* El Watan*). It's all the easier for me since we are friends, who I've translated and published in the Apic editions collection, "Poems of the World" [Algeria]. I won't get into your biobibliography here. After all, readers can buy your collections in Algiers and get to know you a little. The three of us had lunch, discussed poetry, translation, politics, Covid, cooking, friends. A good time. Of course, there was no question of doing an interview and breaking the ambiance! But I had promised to write, so I prepared nine questions that I sent to Pierre and Charles, giving them a little time to answer. Charles answered first, in English (I translated his answers, except for the third question, which he translated himself), Pierre answered in French, a bit later due to health issues. They did not consult each other before writing their responses.* [For this English version, Pierre translated himself and Charles translated the introduction and the questions.*]*

1. Let's start with New York. It's a city that has made more than one poet dream, just to mention Lorca and Adonis. You live there: what can you say?

Charles Bernstein: I'm a native of New York. My mother grew up in what they called "Flatbush" in her day, now Midwood, in Brooklyn. She was born in 1921. As I write this, I am looking at a memorial candle for her; she died this day three years ago. My father, born in 1901, hails from the Lower East Side of Manhattan. Both were children of immigrants. Most of my life was spent on the Upper West Side of Manhattan. On one of New York's hottest days, in 2013, we moved to Brooklyn. My mother, who achieved her dream of moving to Manhattan when she got married just a few months after end of the war in 1945, was appalled I was moving back: "Aren't you going to miss the city?," she said in way that was both sarcastic and concerned. I am so immersed in New York that it's hard to imagine any outside. Today, picking up my car from a repair shop, I drove to Eighth Avenue in Sunset Park – not so far from where Pierre lives. I had heard about a dumpling store, which turned out to be a tiny place on a back street with two tables and a walk-up window. I bought two bags of frozen dumplings and got the scallion pancakes and egg roll hot, to eat in the car. The taste of Madeline has nothing on this. I walked up and down Eighth Avenue: it was so very like similar places in China I'd visited. The streets were packed: fish, vegetables, clothing, and electronics were for sale from stores that flowed onto the sidewalk. Everyone was wearing a mask; in my neighborhood people don't wear masks outside anymore. I had never walked through this neighborhood before. Its homey unfamiliarity is at the heart of what New York is for me, what make me feel — *here, I belong,* at least in my own fashion.

Pierre Joris: I fell in love with New York at the end of August 1967 when I first landed at JFK. I am still totally in love with this city. Though I have often been unfaithful —I lived for years in London, Paris, Constantine, San Diego — upon returning to New York she always received me with open arms. It's where I am, it's where I'll stay. What André Breton & his friends we're looking for in their pre-situationist *dérives*, i.e. drifts through Paris, I experience here by just walking our everyday streets. In a 15 minute stroll through Bay

Ridge, my quarter in southwest Brooklyn, I pass through the ancient Scandinavian level of immigration, overlaid by the new Russian & Bulgarian arrivals mixed with the Latino/as, to arrive in "Little Beirut" where shortly I'm going to go to eat the best Foul Mudammas in the world in a Yemeni restaurant, & when walking home I'll pick up an organic Korean or Mexican dinner. As I'm hungry I'm talking food but I could just as well have talked poetry or art & the same richness & diversity would have shown itself — this weekend I'm going to visit an exhibition that juxtaposes Kandinsky & Etel Adnan, the friend who just disappeared, & / or I'll go to MoMa to see work by Sophie Taeuber-Arp, Joseph E. Yoakum or my Moroccan friend with whom I collaborated around texts by Mohammed Khaïr-Eddine, namely Yto Barrada. And while crossing New York I'll have in my ears some of the 250 languages regularly spoken here. And on my way home maybe I'll stop to see a poet friend —hi Charles! —to talk poetry and poetics …

2. The pandemic has caused havoc in the United States as well as in all the world. How did you live through these difficult days?

Bernstein: I turned 70 at the height of the pandemic, drinking a bottle of gin on my back porch that Saturday night, imagining all the people I would have been with. New York was in a fever pitch. We avoided going out. I was lucky to have recently retired, not to be taking care of children, and to have plenty of space, my books, my computer. I was able to continue with my work. I completed the manuscript for *Topsy-Turvy* that first covid Spring. I was able to sort through scores of boxes of books I had taken home from my Penn office. I spent more time cooking — and never so well – coming out 10 pounds heavier (I know I am not alone). But I felt acutely the loss of a social world – of gatherings, dinners, drinks, readings, openings, performance … While Zoom may be a necessary convenience, it often left me feeling more alienated; I prefer the phone and email/texts. It was an enormous pleasure to do a live reading last month, and at a spectacular space, the Morgan Library, their first live event after closing for the pandemic. Then again, Carroll Gardens, where I live, came back sooner than a lot of New York, so it was possible, after the worst, to shop locally, to go for walks, and to see neighbors in the street. One of my first visitors was Pierre – we sat far apart in the backyard and talked. My immediate neighborhood had relatively low covid rates compared to other neighborhoods in walking distance. Class difference was never more conspicuous or deadly. But we did not have the mask and vaccine resistance that has become part of the Republican Party agenda. And we had, in New York, a vibrant, courageous group of healthcare, transit, food service, and delivery workers who made things more manageable, as you long as you stayed out of harm's way, which was not easy. I met Susan over 50 years ago and we have been through a lot together. No better fortune than to be together during these days.

Joris: Like just about everybody else we stayed cloistered at home for a long long time… for me as a writer & for my wife, Nicole Peyrafitte, as an artist, this has paradoxically allowed us to concentrate on current work & to start new projects. Outside, disaster, death: as you know New York was very badly hit — at night, for weeks and even months, nothing but the continuous noise of sirens & ambulances. And then, walking through the streets close to where we live, the refrigeration trucks parked in front of the funeral homes to help absorb the surplus of dead people. But then, here's another of New York's magnificent aspects: the city is a series of islands & bays, & thus has vast amounts of beaches, coastal walks & so on. We would go out very early in the morning by car in order to undertake long walks along various seashores or around Jamaica Bay, which allowed us to keep some sanity, before returning home to work.

3. Has your poetry been adversely affected? Do you think it has had repercussions for American poetry?

Bernstein: Crisis, dislocation, suffering, disorientation, panic, illness, injustice — for me these are poetry's homeground (*el watan*). It's not apparent how the pandemic has affected American poetry. I would hope it might foment a reframing, as with the environmental crisis, to a non-US-centric perspective. But the odds are stacked against that.

Joris: Of course it did. But that's difficult to evaluate right now. I had, nearly as a joke, promised my editor not to send him a Covid-themed manuscript. But of course the whole experience entered the writing. As it will enter the writing of writers here and elsewhere. Here in the US this virus was shadowed by another virus called Trump —maybe even more nefarious — & we had to fight on two fronts at the same time. And we're not done yet: Covid is still with us & so is fascist racism.

4. When the pandemic began, Trump was in power and I know you were totally depressed by his presidency. Now that a Democratic president has taken over, what's changed?

Bernstein: Like everyone I know, I am scared by the ever-rightward march of the Republican Party and the immediate threat to our constitutional republic. A frightening number of voters want to keep America in the incapable hands of white ethnic Christians, many of whom live in sparsely populated enclaves, held together by community bonds and fundamentalist faith that makes a moral imperative of preventing those who do not share their worldview from having a fair share of political power. Trump's slogan, purportedly about the 2020 election, "Stop the Steal," is true when understood as *stop the steal of our country from people like you: it's our country, not yours.* As the they chanted in Charlottesville, "Jew will not replace us," where *Jew/you* is the meant as the cruelest smear of a vast mosaic refugees, African- and Asian-Americans, queers, Mexicans, Arabs, and anyone else *not like me.* These *volk* are violently opposed to the principle of "one person one vote," even beyond the inequities written into the constitution: the composition of the senate (two representatives from each state) and the electoral college system that allows the loser of an election, such as Trump and Bush II, to take state power. The opposition is strong, but often undermined by dancing to the Republican bullets (remember those old Westerns where the drunken thug would shoot at the feet of some half-drunken citizen, making him dance to dodge the bullets). The Democrats in Congress can only do so much given the fact that New York State's over 19 million people have the same number of senators as Wyoming's just over 1/2 million. Wyoming has about the same population as mostly Black Washington, D.C., which, appallingly, has no vote in federal elections. (Brooklyn has over 2½ million people. We should be our own state.) Throughout my lifetime, the U.S. has proclaimed itself a beacon of democracy; it's never been that, but at times it's aspired to it, or some of us have. At the same time, even if our elections allowed for a more representative government, even if more people voted, we might still see success by a globally robust right. Fear, stoked by revanchist and atavistic forces, can produce startlingly xenophobic power plays; and those once crushed by the boot will often use their newly acquired power to polish their new boots so brightly they can see their faces in the leather.

Joris: We actively fought for these elections & it was a great relief when Biden won. He's doing a lot of good work but I am very afraid that the example of Donald Trump and what he represents constitutes a major, major danger for American democracy. The "great lie" of *stop to steal* (go directly to Hitler's *Mein Kampf* to see the fascists' insistence on the need for such "great lies") fills the hyper-paranoid white racists with energy because they know that in another decade or so they will be a minority in this country. And they will do anything to keep power. A *coup d'éta*t cannot be excluded. They already tried to do this on sixth of January 2021 & if it didn't work that time nothing says that it won't work next time. Republicans have changed any number of laws in the various states where they hold power, giving them permission to change the results of the elections if they don't like them. This on top of the fact that at a national level the power structure already gives immense power to the small states (in the south and west) compared to states with much greater share of the population like New York or California. The electoral dice are loaded. Scary.

5. Coming back to poetry, you participate in numerous readings in the United States and around the world. Do you think poetry readings affect your writing? What is the role of voice in a poem's construction?

Bernstein: Poetry readings are fundamental for poetry and such readings/performances produce versions of the poems as significant as their printed counterparts. A poem is not one idealized "text" but an array of multiple and possibly contradictory versions, none of which has priority. To this end, in 2005 Al Filreis and I co-founded PennSound, which makes available, free, sound files of poetry readings (and videos) – the largest such archive (and mostly in English), going back a century. (Go to writing.upenn.edu/pennsound.) I also edited a book on this topic, *Close Listening: Poetry and the Performed Word*, published by Oxford University Press in 1998. Since that time, there has been a burgeoning interest in "sound studies," including poetry performances

Joris: Essential. One of the major reasons for my decision to come to the United States & to write in English was exactly my admiration for beat poetry & it's connections with music, especially with jazz. Once here, I discovered a further range of poetries connected with voice, that of Charles Olson among others. What gives, controls and changes the rhythm of the line is breath — & thus the whole body of the poet is central to the elaboration of the text while public readings become central for poetic creation. In fact it's always been like that except for a few print-monopolized centuries in Europe — & I have for example always admired the Maghreb for having over several millennia known how to keep those two great modes, the written & the oral, function simultaneously while strengthening each other.

6 Do you see differences between American poetry and that of other countries? Are there ties between American poetry and that of other countries?

Bernstein: There is no poet more American than me. And yet the American is just a part of my identity, and it can often be a suffocating part. I am deeply inspired by, and am in the tradition of, the great 18th and 19th century American Protestant (& protesting) philosophers, poets, and novelists. Like them, I find many of the dominating cultural and political attitudes extremely parochial. It's been a lifesaver for me to be in deep exchange with many poets and translators from Europe, Asia, and South America. The new issue of *boundary 2*, which includes you and Pierre, charts some of these relationships. While crucial to recognize cultural and social differences, at the same time our *potential* affinities allow for necessary syncretism you across state lines and language barriers.

Joris: Of course & happily so. The same poetry everywhere would be deeply boring! One important aspect of my work is to bring the poetries from other countries over here via translation. I spent a lot of time (time I could have spent writing more poems) translating (you for example, Habib, but also Kerouac into French, & Paul Celan & many others into English) & to gather with friend Jerome Rothenberg the *Poems for the Millennium* anthologies. For me, one of the goals of poetry is also to create community. As Pound put it: "poetry is news that stays news." Given the jamming of & interference with so many communication channels (overweening buzz of social media, disappearance of local newspapers, with all the major media in the hands of the large monopolistic capitalist conglomerates), it is more important than ever to find other ways & means. Poetry can be one of these.

7. Is there today a major trend in poetry writing in the U.S., or are there multiple paths being drawn? What can you say?

Bernstein: Well, the *major* ones that I *see* I don't much like and I may be too old to catch the ones unseen, the minor, where the action surely is. I always hated when older writers would say they are looking backwards, but I am, reading lots of "historical" work that I had missed or not had the time for, as well as keeping up with long-time loves. As I told you when you and Pierre came over for BBQ, I just discovered Muhyiddin Ibn 'Arabi (in a new English translation) and was knocked out. I do follow new poetry and am open to and for it, but not sure I want to categorize it. I was happy, but wary, about editing, with Tracie Morris, a collection of "the best" "experimental" writing, 2016, for Wesleyan University Press, despite disliking the terms *best* and *experimental*. I made it a rule not to include anyone who had published a book before the early 1990s, to eliminate my immediate company; that focused my attention and there was a great deal I liked. And working with Tracie was great – she is not just an "out of the box" thinker, sometimes I think she doesn't even countenance the box. I think you can say I am avoiding your question, possibly successfully. Younger U.S. poets are under a lot of pressure to pledge allegiance to a better world order, which is admirable, but perhaps undercuts a kind of aesthetic abandon I like: you know, *Fleurs du Mal*, and all that jazz. But that pressure is not new, whether from the right or the left or, most debilitatingly, the center. (I'd call it the *tyranny of the center*.) People now talk about "cancel" culture: the liberal mainstream organs of literary taste have always been that. *Poetry will out* and in unexpected ways. I've done what I could; now I am trying to both make space and get out of the way.

Joris: Several paths, no doubt, but with one major tendency which is that of the creative writing programs & departments on our university campuses — these in the main rather sad-sack & reactionary because essentially based on the little lyrical musick of the individual expressing ("self-expression" being the impoverished aim) his/her fears, angst, etc. It is also the professionalization of poetry: you end up with a degree in writing & you go on to teach the same thing, creative writing, in another factory producing "poets."

Now, in the big cities, but also in the great plains, in the mountains, there is massive actual lived experience & many poets who work on a poetry deeply connected to the outside world & not just to their bruised egos. I am certain that in today's very difficult situation of the US — & of the world — new poetries will emerge. The matter of ecology & the matter of politics (white supremacy, systematic racism) are two very important engines here. There are, for example, very powerful Native American poetries like that of, say, Layli Long Soldier (Oglala Sioux) & Nathalie Diaz (Mojave) & many others asking essential questions.

8. You are both published in Algeria, what impression does that make on you?

Bernstein: That's the way I want my work to move. It makes me feel alive.

Joris: It feels a little bit like a home-coming! As you know, Habib, because that's where we met in 1976 or 7, I worked for three years in Constantine & Algeria has always remained close to me. I hope that my book & Charles' & all the others that you will publish in your series will open a small window on the world for Algerian readers. Let's have a dialogue, a trialogue, a multilogue. There is need for mixing it all up, because, as I wrote long ago, "purity is the root of all evil." Let's creolize the world, as Édouard Glissant proposed.

9. If an international festival of contemporary poetry was organized in Algeria, would you come if invited?

Bernstein: I'd be on the next plane.

Joris: Hold on just a second — lemme close my suitcase!

[tear sheet from original publication: http://writing.upenn.edu/epc/ authors/bernstein/interviews/Tengour.pdf]

from *Men in Suits*

Norman Fischer

When shall I come to the top of that same hill?

You climb it nowe, look how we labor

Methinks the ground is even

No, horrible steep. Do you hear the sea?

No

What, then your other senses grow imperfect when your eyes can't see?

Yes it may be methinks thy voice is altered and thou speakest in better phrase and manner than thou didst

Y'are much deceived in nothing am I changed but in my garments

Cracks in doors.... Feverish times bring feverish places

      hosts arrive, guests soon come...

            Takes the pace of temperament, I'm as I am changing
              clothes, wolf in sheep's
                  Men prey on them but then the male's caught in gap
                  between them

All terrified of their mom   great darkness then before birth

---

His mother was prostitute w/heart of gold she looked after him he sat in her room with clients who were kind to him killer killed mother dreaming sees her face large smiling at him comforted he's tough guy goes to war becomes cop toughly wounded—

            later[there's no later in this kind of world where there's wounding/wounder/wounded it seems there's seeming time sticks but immediately blasts time blasts no time then in that in

This

Kind

Of world..... *[the one they're in but we're not in it]*

He years later encounters the man at end of long involved crime scene case he is greedy wealthy guy in control of dark city real estate always the real estate controlling cities then money then countryside manipulating loans deals banks nothing nothing/smashing and building's best business solely crooked manipulating spacetime's funny money he's that/ he finds him in cave, tunnel of some sort, maybe old construction site for building some building he sees him holds him shoots him in these shows people constantly

shooting *[wham body hurled across space sudden then still soundblast decisive no process no ambiguity no nuance whambock flying body shot dead/ story ends*

One, the other, that part of plot done but more killings to come

In another/ drug scene he creeps into house very fancy very modern LA house very nice up in hills bushes large long hallways lots of gunmetal matte greengray cabinets floortoceiling so on he's in back room at hallway's long end has gun but holds up hands with gun in hand the cop also has gun who's gonna shoot first criminal Black guy from Haiti gangs says I gonna trust you still has gun though but hands up gonna trust you but cop also Black the Haiti guy's shot his cousin in Haiti but now in LA where money rules and he has money he gets off he has no worries he can be criminal no worries though in LA if there's money you have money play ball with DA and so on so he's got nerve confident puts up hands with gun in hand says gonna trust you but the Black cop shoots him anyway dead cause he knows no other way to get justice but take it in own hands when you have gun in them you got what justice takes/justice it's the final move…

Battered buttered abuse. She shouts at them they can't hear her are in another show,another channel. She's in Norway his father senile, maybe a painter, yes, painter painting sere Norway snowy hills trees lovely Norway tree remembering all the cruelty in the quiet, but she flies away on high above all that her soul's got wings she takes up from top of painted hill in Norway[does this in th painting part of theater piece written by Black woman about flying off flying away into heaven there's no else except this shithole racist world not worth the trouble of saving so she flies]disappears elsewhere gone pure nothing it's.

Later when her mother is located she tries to forgive her but no she's unforgivable she's doing this/drinks whole bottle down/asks men for money says she would like to fuck the men but not for the money.

no she

    simply needs money this and that a

    girl

       must love this is her mother she thinks I also must be
unreliable in just this way inside herself she feels this way but can't say
so in herself she acts out of course she does and the brutal men remain
at attention ready for such eventualities.

if there weren't flesh in the first place

if there weren't preferences/need to eat/run away from bad guys raping
eating you

weren't world to mKe contact with

if words weren't hoNey

if the finality weren't final/melting[*'melting'* can't be state or condition a
thing is in]nor superior nor inferior nor equal

    When in disappearing

    flashburst

       starts to shoot

    Who can doubt the shooters' guns

      sold in legitimate business also prisons to lock them up but
        shooting's OK

       war only necessary, self defense/ th' right to shoot even
yourself/ we provide means/shoot husband wife child/protect against dark
man coming at you on street or into your house or yard

one heatmoment is all *worldshakes* blasts

Is normal[is all all]

Freedom, its price!

Plots no longer as before
include crack cocaine dealers
in inner cities or Mexican gangs
shipping drugs or manufacturing them
instead mental illness the people manic
in face of swooning world
bad economics/drumbeat
of diminishment/across the road
confections/derailments
built on linguistic abnormalities
no words to be said to faces
no one there//

(King rages on heath/self unravels)

How king gets th' way he is he gets it by birth by intrigue authority
cheaply in intrigue by birth and crook by hook or crook rages on heath it
was fake superiority fake authority fake magnanimity one who cares can't
say one who says won't care Carpe diem

when

king[*like in wal king or stal king or bal king or thin king*]

arrived in king dom

kingdom woke up like hills at dawn before in night they skeot[hikls slept]
{no king langurgab breakf-wnss;;[';

Danger for holes there

Made by gopher or fox skun king stumbled there

(No atheists no airheads in foxholes they say)

"No arhythmia in foxholes"

—- not going to church — ceremonies there to take seriously —

Children hollowed out insincerity they mean what they say just now getting used to language not knowing it means opposite of what words say not knowing this fall into king's foxhole

    4 foxes there mommy and daddy and grandma and 6 baby foxes there/foxes needle-snouted/wisewily foxesfixes/bits it's natural to perish.....nature's brutal

In. In.// In foxhole fixes there.

Connecticut muffins
Over obdurate scene
My offthecharts emotionality
Can't deduce from former
        Frictions
      A fiction
    That stands for my life[by which I apprehend such quicksilver

Outside quotation marks
'What kind interruptions?'
Is static   In utopias we believe in we think

One's 'hard' of 'hearing'
   Yes — object thought —
Can't betray your hobbyhorse
    Expecting to ride

'Actually he's up in space'
'Where food doesn't occupy time'

There and the. The detective emerged from the squalid found
Body covered in green mold
The plot of Lear
Denigrate Potemkin Russians don't care anyway
'Truth' unknown to them

Patient acceptance of all this that's failed to be produced is isn't inside/
outside fixes or outside them (who only want food small bits of money)
[like she says her mother has no quid pro quo there's no quid pro quo]
Serious devices.   In serious times.   Define or

      make it be

          as is.   Just. *[this thingmoment asis stresss/*
                            instress/inscape somesuch

Searching for solutions so what we wish to be do's so but this not
possible nor conceivable in material world as is, some faulty words here
fix em/but can't fix em that ship sailed uncle Homer

          fix as *stay in place* as in place "in" sist/spire/fluence

        under the....

"Little *'the'*" as in

        In?   fixed it there as one this one
                            [one being anyone not a one

Patiently accepting it's not there

Five Poems from *Three Four Five* and Poems from *Pieces*

Hank Lazer

i thought
she would
run out the clock

gracefully
she did not
i wouldn't say
that her death-path

haunts me
the entrapment
the lack of choice
& no control
sun-faced buddha   moon-faced buddha

12.26.2021
Duncan Farm

truth is neither
known nor
held   cloud

cover in early
morning & a distant
rooster crows
three dogs 2 4 & 14

at rest in different
metrics of remaining
life   the new telescope
human curiosity
in search of beginnings

12.27.2021
Duncan Farm

i don't know
for whom poetry
remains

of interest
this space
of being
to which

i have given
my life
all to sense
a hidden
rhythm

1.1.2022 (4)
For Donald Revell

let me tell you
how this book
began

years ago
in a little village
or big city in Russia
or Lithuania or Ukraine

a man named Henry
was the mayor & a very
learned & curious person
he died in America
before i was born

1.9.2022 (3)

is being
itself
the quicksand

you are made
to thrash around
in   place it
gently under your

tongue   she said
it's *mishegoss*
but she had seen
the pogroms
when she was very young

1.13.2022 (2)

from PIECES

11.12.2021

each
& every
shall have a say
*

thinking
is the real
dancing its way
inward
*

say
what
*

11.12.2021   Duncan Farm

delirium's
insistent
sibling
*

vowels
collide
clotted
cream
*

won't be
summed up
*

becoming
something
*

have you
found it
mystery

suffering
miracle
of being
incarnate
*
all
go
through it
*
a light
too bright
*

by his very
being
he summoned
goodness
from others
*
sing
the idiosyncrasy
of this
as it whispers
through
time
*
until
it casts
a shadow
*
warmed
by morning light
sun
above the tree line
*
as he said
some time ago
we wonder now
if there will be

a future
*

world
made of his mind
is it this one
is it that one
*

no
not
what thinking knows
*

i wish to bring you
to that back country
pasture   hillside
& old farmhouse
*

remote
depends upon
your willingness
*

all the buddhas
past present & future
sit with you
*

time's
indecipherable
rhythm
*

no theme
no plan
proceeding
as is
momentary
guest
in the house
of being

from *Residential Poems*

☆

Lee Duggan

taller roads
 bend to toll house
      higher than trees

            spacing
            all
                  these things
        to take me
              home

                        deposit
                           grit faced
                                 doll head
                           stray germination
                                    clung
                        to millstone
                           chalk white dragon
                                       blood
                  naked through hemlock

perk the nerves & glide

chaste & fleshy
taper through stem
to deeper systems
wicca
taproot
blotched ovular
tips
resonating Saturn
beyond seed & ritual

curvature riverline
point & drift
stripped ripples
making me
a virtual tower

the top forest reduced to swamp
tumble
lumber recovery
left to rot

snakebite
hum acute noted
hold & respond

under bare arms
blistered lips
a burning sensation

sirens without sound

the dappled alder
too soon to bud
branching

what can be
too soon to

to have known

alight
                        laying the ground for
                                    ditches & marsh

                a range of woody specimens
            hawthorn ragged at the edges
                            willow white downy crack
                so many types of wax cap

        drunk with
                    sweet woodruff stinking hellebore
                                & lesser celandine

                    potion of recall
                            reducing drystone boulders to pebbles

            pun on
                            all those trees
                    quick to dry micro fibre
                        & spare socks

                    where slate stairs form the entrance
                                            chestnut alley
                            & after rain occasional chanterelle

                                        riff
                                distance   a jazz solo

                        left to chance

        out
                here
            off-void
                        moonshine
                            shimmer a music of this
                                        chained
                                        comedown

                    smooth
                small things
                            in order of truth

        low in valley shadow
                        just past focus
                a note swirls

                    backfills the space down river
                        obstruction
                                motion or gesture outside ourselves

                            no talk of whirlpools just circular currents
        a good place to get in

                too high
                            they left
                                    high to close your eyes
                            too tight

                    bound sheer
                        to every rock face
                                    crevice or other
                                        mechanical
                            no reply
                                    words
                lost to
                        slimy underfoot
                sharp noted
            scenery gathered
        city lights
                kestrels
            & poetry

                        once sacred miss-information
                        getting through blocked lines
                        that voice & wires of disconnect

                                kept me

forever against

pull

further the horizon

can almost reach mud

waders & gulls eye me

keep limbs moving

back to warm dinners & bed tImes

semi-permanent domicile

all the activity for living

in static virtual spaces

where we perform being

physical forms of home

sheltered in picture books

find refuge off the footpath

where signs are with the seasons

& a ringing in one ear

another figure

as this body turns

salient from space

outline sharpens through

clenched view

dusk lets stray rays seep storm

confused cloudburst & ringing

overwhelmed vices

& out of hope

we are all washed down river

my

my

my/

this

body
bands face

blood echos
chest

history of outward
bound
journeys
& carrion figures

struck randomly

rooked up
shouting
no real sounds to take meaning

just

irregular line breaks
inhalation & triggers

higher trace tributaries
spring through tarmac
shiver as village crosses river

on lower levels liquids transmute

safe in 4 main elements
4 types of matter
sediment pills & pockets

leave alchemy to google NHS

the apparatus
now you
then this

The Infant King

George Salis

With the advent of morning, the widow queen's labial folds finally crowned the face of the infant king, and her engorged clitoris resembled a coronal ruby, the first of many jewels. The omnipresence of compressed screams made the infant king feel as though he were being issued upon a battlefield, omens to his ears, and as he was pushed farther, his face the center of a fleshy flower, all he discerned through the clotted pollen of his mother's amniotic fluid was the beckoning hands of a midwife, no cavalry charging toward him, no siege weapons hurling meteors of flame, thus his face became calm, although resigned, and when he was expelled from the birth canal, plucked and held aloft by the midwife, instinct caused his petite hands to clasp his own umbilical cord, the definitive connection to his private kingdom. With awe and tenderness, the midwife sliced it, causing his hands to release and his arms to spread outward, and she knotted it, creating a bulging third eye, chatoyant-pupiled. After a pat on the back forced the fluids of his former realm from his mouth and nostrils, he was washed and handed to his mother.

Even while covered by eau de Nil cloth, the magnetism of his mother's nipples played upon his lips. Her finger, with a nail like a setting moon in a pink sky, descended toward him and he grasped it with a little hand that had been sculpted for the scepter. Her eyes watered as she looked upon this miraculous bundle, this sinless godsend. The infant king saw her irises as two sapphire circles, more jewels, and their dazzle made him smile, but then he frowned. Looming near his mother was the uncle, his face a chiaroscuro dominated by darkness, giving him half a gray eye, a beetroot-colored cluster of veins within the sclera, and half an upper row of russet teeth. Since before the infant king existed, it seemed, his breathing was in sync with his mother's, but the surprise caused by this figure, this invader, made his strawberry heart hesitate, and his breathing was untethered, adopting an irregular rhythm. His mother lifted him closer to her face, and the air pouring from her nostrils soothed him. She inhaled, taking it back, and began to form that air into song: *Mon trésor, mon John, sombre dans un profond sommeil....* In the seconds before his thin lids closed, the infant king searched in vain for the second face, the disembodied features of the uncle.

***

When he awoke, in the palm of his velvet basinet, he fought the urge to cry. The lack of song, of his mother's breathing, distressed him. He needed her, yearned for the protective dome of her stomach. He belonged beneath it, in his uterine kingdom, communicating with the goddess by way of vibrations, echoed feelings, mysterious forces that encoded implicit language. How simple it was to rule then, how simple to exist. Now, he was forced to cry, and with the whole of his little body he did, like a broken bellows. By the time his lungs could squeeze the air no longer, he was still alone.

He positioned himself so that he could peer over the basinet's lip. That's when he spotted her, his mother in her expansive bed, and he released a hopeless wail. Her body was the color of fog and her skin was pustulating. He attempted to crawl toward her, reaching across the divide in futility, when he noticed a shadowed hump and looked down. There was the uncle, petrified upon the floor, mouth agape and filled with bubbling sores, his eyes locked into arching creases, as though wishing something away. A pillow, the fabric decorated with golden vines and pale flowers, was clamped in the tombstones of his hands.

Having fought the restlessness of his limbs, the infant king relaxed, laid on his back, and tuned into his partly psychic umbilical stump. Like an owl with a thousand and one eyes, he was able to scrutinize the entirety of his new dominion, the size of which was finite but without boundary: he witnessed a farmer face down in a turnip field, Philippe de Vitry rotting over the notes for his *Ars nova notandi*, a powdered harlot strewn naked amongst gold coins, an obscure philosopher who had been one thought away from defining the exact nature of the human mind, a slumped drunkard gripping an empty flask behind a tavern, a merchant's daughter on the floor of her bedroom with a silver comb stuck in her hair, an artisan fallen upon an unfinished block of marble from which Venus' leg protrudes, a jester next to a spilled chamber pot with his vermillion trousers around his ankles, Levi Ben Gershon tangled in a bed of flowers in his back yard, a crude prototype of Jacob's staff on his chest, with which he had attempted to measure the angular distant between stars. So many bodies, all vessels of decay. Was this his first nightmare as a burdened king, the mysterious annihilation of his citizenry?

He heard the semi-arrhythmic patter of naked footsteps but could see no one. A heavy creak indicated the door of his quarters was opening. The use of his stump's power seemed to have exhausted it, so he pushed his small body upward and saw a cloaked toddler standing by the door, next to which was the blackened body of the midwife, and before the infant king could cry again, the toddler put a finger to his lips, then, bowing slightly, said, "Youw Machesty…." While the infant king's navel acted as an ear of translation, the toddler explained that a hyper-saprogenic plague of the most discriminatory kind had killed all but the infants and a few toddlers who could pass as such. Hearing the toddler speak was somewhat comforting, unlike all the foreign sounds he had encountered since being banished from his mother. Yet he still longed for the enveloping swishes of blood flow, digestion, cartilaginous joints, and all other minutiae of bodily function that used to stimulate his developing cochleae. Even though conversations with his mother had at times felt one-sided, he could never forget how he pushed, stroked, kicked, prodded, and kissed the amniotic sac like a call bell when he required melodious comfort, like an instrument when he felt the need for artistic expression, like the nape of a loyal servant who could simply acknowledge his existence, even if all of it was as close and as far as the act of prayer. Now, looking at this toddler in his composed eyes, though the words he had spoken would mean the nightmare was true, the infant king knew he could trust him.

***

The infants were survivors of what came to be thought of as a supernatural cleansing. They realized that they wouldn't grow. They could feel it, the lack of ache in their limbs, the numbing stasis of their perpetual forms. Out of all these orphans, the infant king knew it most deeply, understood it as his first test, a challenge worthy of his royal intellect. As the hours of that first day passed, he and his populace grew used to their stunted bodies. With persistence, they learned to walk upright, but the proletarian infants still crawled on their hands and knees, which the infant king deemed a divine-willed hierarchy, the impervious structure of this cradle of life. Clad in a silk onesie and ermine cape, he spent the second day upon his throne, feet dangling or swinging back and forth. A crown had been forged for him, decorated with diamonds, rubies, emeralds, and amethysts. The weight of it pressed into his skull. In his left hand he gripped a golden rattle as his scepter, the bejeweled head of which contained the teeth of his pillow-wielding uncle. And with the index finger of his right hand he massaged his pudding-soft temple, attempting to tolerate the grating pleas of each drooling and snot-bubbling citizen.

They wobbled toward him one by one while Clovis, his toddler advisor, stood nearby, fiddling with his fingers behind his back. The infant king's protruding stump, which he sometimes tapped through his clothing, facilitated the translation of their various cries and wails, postnatal sounds absorbed by the tapestries hanging from the walls, muffled by the stained glass windows and castle stones. They mourned for their mothers most of all. The infant king explained, with a finger in his nostril, that the plague was a sign from above. A liberated generation was created here, to begin anew. Clovis nodded and explained the similarities between now and a genocidal flood many histories ago. The infant king shook his rattle over his head. Then he said they were the chosen ones, to forever hold the form of innocence. He lathered a large golden ball of mucus on the throne's armrest. More came to His Majesty's steps, some far enough to reach up and kiss the soles of his feet, which tickled and made him kick the air and spread his toes. Most of the babies wore fabrics of motley quality, including turnip sacks, while some were nude, forced to feel the cracking of their vitreous skin in the cold, the searing of their fuzzy scalps beneath the heat, grateful for the temporary shelter in this throne room, for the braziers alight and flickering down the length of the walls. A robust baby limped forward, suffering from a kind of scoliosis so that his nape nearly formed a peak. As with the others before him, he cried for want of matriarchal milk, the hum and the backrub, the warmth of belly and breasts. Seeing how the citizen's hump was nearly mammary in shape, the infant king barely stifled an effervescent laugh, then, fingers in his wet mouth, he told him that these he would have to do without. Nodding, Clovis said that they would all live a more Spartan life than what they've known thus far. The infant king made a fist, studied it, and said that this way of life will harden them, bring forth more calculated humors. This will also apply to the infants who had expressed envy over the aristocrats' silver pacifiers, their abundance of blankets, and their jugs of lukewarm milk. Besides the urgency of personal plights, whether the plague had been an endemic or a pandemic remained to be determined. Fears of barbaric Goliaths storming the kingdom had spread as quickly as any sickness. All His Majesty could say was that he was procuring several infantries for defensive purposes, testing the prototypes of innovative siege weapons, including bottle-nipple cannons and dirty diaper catapults.

Despite his composure, the infant king was overwhelmed by the chaos and responsibility of it all. And, when his subjects had left, he shook his rattle at Clovis to indicate that his goblet of milk should be warmed and his basinet prepared for naptime. Then the infant king swallowed, muting his rattle, when shadow-hidden creatures emerged and hobbled, tripped, and scratched toward his throne. Cycloptic babies with rachitic deformities of the thorax, acardiac babies bean-eared by microtia and insect-limbed by phocomelia, anencephalic and hydrocephalic newborns with aprosopia, all approached, many having been forced to learn physics-defying methods of perambulation. Clamping his nose with thumb and forefinger, Clovis stepped forward and extended a flat hand. "Stoyp dere!" The leaking and boiling liquids of their barely alive bodies had humidified the throne room, stained and caked the rug beneath them.

The infant king's umbilical stump swelled and throbbed with a bombardment of psychic pain: *I am cursed. Death has forgotten me, sickness has not. I come from the surface of a warped mirror, my sister from a rippled puddle. Calcified brains. I was forced from a star-shaped birth canal, grated by coarse labia. Fungal skin. I drag my skull with a leash of veins. To breathe is torture. My body is more viral matter than it is me. I exist only because filth takes the form of life. Liquid skeletons. I survived the Judas Cradle, my mother did not. Mutations at fertilization. I ate my twin brother while in the womb. Marbled pupils. My toenails peel away like the petals of a dead flower. Maggots live in my genitals, gnats in my nasal cavity. Telophasic hearts. I am bacteria welded to the lifeless root of humanity.*

Itchy and sweaty, the infant king shrieked and instinctively grabbed at his ears. The noise of their thoughts became dissonant, morphed into demoniac echolalia, echoing with pustulating pullulations that pulled the left hemisphere of his brain, with elusive ululations that lulled the right hemisphere, his skull a psychedelic citadel on the precipice of sepsis. He pinched his umbilical stump and it ceased. Readjusting his crown, he shouted for them to leave. He picked the rattle up from his lap and shook it, the sound like a medley of bones falling into a barren well, and his advisor shooed them with his arms. At first it seemed as though they wouldn't leave, but then the convulsive crowd trudged backward, as if repeating all their contorted movements in reverse, and were subsumed once more into the shadows.

"Sowy, Youw Machesty," said Clovis, kneeling at the side of the throne with his head bowed.

The infant king wiped the phlegm from his upper lip and flicked it in his direction. *All is forgiven.* Then they both turned their heads toward the shadows, hearing a steady whimper, beneath which was the sound of scuttling. Something materialized. A bright red, premature baby. It crawled like a centipede on the tips of its fingers and toes and its twisted head dragged against the floor. The fluids that leaked from its mouth and other orifices left a limacine trail. Patches of black hair sprouted from its skin, the aborted beginnings of fleece. Clovis, flecks of the infant king's mucus drying on his forehead, said, "Begoyne!" It collapsed at the first step, trembling before arching its back and becoming motionless, stuck in its warped position. The infant king and his advisor stared. Its eye opened in the manner of a fungal spore sac. Perplexed, the infant king caressed his umbilical stump, trailing the rim with the tip of his finger, and it wrinkled, tuning into the crackly thought patterns of the premature baby:

I speak for them.

The infant king contemplated this. *And what say you?*

Your Majesty is blind.

He squeezed the handle of his rattle. *My sight is ubiquitous.*

To see everything is sometimes to see nothing.

Loosening his grip, he scrutinized this creature, the shape and consistency of its body a blood clot. *What has befallen you?*

I am a being born early so that my mind can sustain a faraway age. I am opposites balanced by an atomic fulcrum.

You are of the cursed, as with the others.

That is true insofar as one is fixated on what the eyes see. Phosphorous foam trickled from its undeveloped tear ducts. *But I am also the beginning and the end.*

***

To ease the infant king into slumber, Clovis told him tales of the world before this one, where the parental gods lived amongst them, and he absorbed every word: Dere wuh wondewfool tings cawed sweets. Dese wuh da food o' da gawds. Yuh cood onwy get 'em by doin' tings en deir favow. N', on me biwfday, uh day dat da gawds howd en high ehsteem, even toh I din't do anyting en da stwict sense of doin' sumtin', I gottuh box o' dem. I hid en me room n' dey smewed suh good I stuffed uhs many uhs I cood enta me noystrils. I poot suh many in dere dat I cood taste 'em chus by smew. Et wuhs uh pweashuh wike no udduh, undil da gawds foynd me wit uh sweet-cuvud noyse, mouf, n' chin. Et even cuvud me cloythes. Deir fuwy made 'em comfiskate whut wuhs weft o' da box, n' I nevuh saw anofuh sweet aftuh. Givef n' takef. Ta dis day, ef I cloyse me eyes n' sniff uh big o' sniff, I can taste 'em aw ovuh uhgayn.

***

The infant king would be deceiving himself if he said he wasn't fearful of the premature baby. Even though he continued to tell himself that the creature was a mad-brained charlatan, there was something ominous about its seething face, a lingering quality that suggested hypnotism. Such was part of the reason he decided to leave the castle and visit his citizenry, for the disguised possibility of finding the premature baby and speaking with him further, but he also wanted to familiarize himself with his subjects, to be an infant of the people, thereby gaining trust and admiration. Before consenting to the journey, Clovis warned him of the fatal nature of the fontanel, explaining how that soft spot was the most tempting target for an assassin. Taking his advice, the infant king ordered a skullcap to be welded to his crown. When the toothless infant blacksmith delivered the armored headwear to His Majesty's throne, he said that anybody going for that weakness will be met with sparks and a bent blade, and his sooty lips made a sucking sound before he added that this here material is the epitome of impregnable.

      The protective crown did little to comfort the infant king as he stepped outside onto the castle's first wall and witnessed with his own eyes the sheer magnitude of his kingdom, the clusters of cottages, the farmed valleys, the distant mountains, and a circle of fire floating above. An agoraphobic queasiness struck his stomach and he doubled over. Clovis hurried to his aid. "Youw Machesty… dwink dis." He brought a flask of milk to his lips. His skin warmed, and he felt lighter, less attached to the world, more inward. Although he yearned to be swaddled, he descended the steps and entered the toy carriage that had been waiting on him. They would be preceded and followed by four infant knights on foalback, who had been recruited by Clovis. The infant coachman produced a couple of clicks from the side of his mouth and the foals, their neighs and whinnies murine in pitch, pulled them through the walls' doors and over the drawbridge. The toddler advisor sat across from the infant king, staring out the window. The infant king kept his gaze to the floor and wondered about his fear of open spaces. He had seen the entirety of his kingdom before, had he not? But now that vista seemed only a hallucination. The infant coachman whipped the foals for greater speed and their elastic hooves squeaked. Feeling the bumps of the road, the infant king tried to relax into the seat's cushion, then closed his eyes and attempted to tune into his stump. He could see the myriad veins in his lids, the passage of phantoms, but nothing more. While Clovis spied a skein of pink and featherless hatchlings, the infant king felt the stump beneath his shirt and came away with a foul yellow discharge stuck to the tip of his finger, which he wiped on the underside of his leg. Had the thought patterns of the premature baby been blighted, had his lame body been contagious? They began to pass an increasing number of spine-arched and skull-cracked skeletons that cast an entanglement of shadows into the carriage. Parents and relatives, all the ripe dead, had been reduced to these leaden memorials. Clouds of smoke hung over every one, churning viscously. The infant king thought of his mother, a calcium sculpture in the middle of a bed, haloed by the dripping smoke. What would she think of him now that his power was being threatened? How would she have counseled him? Making certain Clovis was unaware, the infant king peered down at his umbilical stump through the collar of his shirt and smothered a cry. The stalk itself was black and brittle, the base sanguine and oozing. "Youw Machesty?" Clovis was looking at him now, and asked if he was feeling well. Refusing to undungeon his emotions, the infant king replied in the affirmative and mentioned the skeletons, how they were a constant reminder of the past, but also the urgency of the future. Clovis nodded and expressed his notion that the bones will be the currency and sustenance of the infant king's reign, they will be both foundation and wall, ceiling and spire. Scholars will look upon the bones during hagiographical research, others will pray at the altar of ribcages in propitiation. The infant king raised his hand and Clovis quieted. The fact that his navel retained the ability of translation, however full of static, was a hopeful sign. Perhaps the degeneration could be reversed. The infant king told Clovis to inform the infant coachman that there would be a change of destination, they will go straight to the darkest slums and mingle with those afflicted with retardation and disfigurement.

They passed the noble lords' castles and the infant serfs who tended to their farmlands, their droves of grazing zygoates, then a group of infant monks and nuns roaming a monastery to the toll of a mysterious and melancholy bell, a swineherd frolicking with his lord's piglets outside a gilded manor, and craftsbabies working upon a half-built cathedral. He had noticed that some of the proletarians were bipedal, which disturbed him. Hours beyond the last cottage, as they wheeled and clomped through mud, they arrived at the shanties of the exiled and destitute. When the infant king exited the toy carriage, he came upon an ashen skeleton, a pair of premature twins sleeping in the cracked-open cranium. Other skeletons held wilting flowers in their eye sockets, candles along vertebral columns, and bric-a-brac between ribs or inside pelvises. These were acts of care and respect, if not outright worship, as Clovis had predicted. The previous skeletons near those castles and manors seemed utterly neglected in comparison, as if those children feared contagion or detested the deceased, grateful for the mass deicide enacted by a still higher will. Clovis and the knights followed the infant king closely as he approached the first shanty. Without a door to knock upon, he leaned forward and peeked inside. On the floor were a multitude of primordial fetuses, no larger than pebbles, gasping and floundering. He swallowed a sickly boiling in his throat. Against the wall, an armless newborn girl cried into the soles of her feet and the infant king's stump translated with much interference: *They just came out of me, it was like I had to poo, and they just came out of me, my darling babies, what can I feed them with, clothe them with, they will never know what it means to be human, what it means to be loved....* The infant king unclasped his ermine cape and wrapped it around the girl's naked back. *There, there. They will never know what it means to be hated, either. They will never know despair, loneliness, loss.* Her crying ceased, but she didn't move. He rubbed her shoulder. *Despondence is but temporary, and our lives must go on.* From his angle he caught sight of a smooth hemisphere between her legs, the other swathed in shadows. There was something tantalizing about it, the vein-riddled part of a den which had spewed embryonic bio-matter. He imagined spreading the hemispheres and crawling headfirst into the heated hole. This desire was followed by feelings of guilt, a strange other-longing, for she was not his mother. When she began to cry again, displacing him from his mental abstraction, he retreated outside.

Larvae swarmed as white mist and he swatted the air when they whirred near his ears and eyes. The infant king looked at Clovis, standing upright in his polished breastplate. The toddler advisor hadn't questioned him about his intentions. His was a silence of obedience. Clovis nodded in a direction behind the infant king, where a crowd had grown. Seeping forth from between the crowd's misshapen limbs was a herd of premature babies, portions of their gooey skeletons exposed to the fecal air, their shrunken skin enflamed with pearlescent bruises. A few of the premature babies were obscured by matted hair, pawing forward like bastard cubs. These creatures were not part of the new race, thought the infant king. What breed of gods had designed them, maintained their inverted pulses? The infant knights unsheathed their swords and the gleaming tips ringed with power. At the raise of the infant king's hand, the knights stood down. Then he spread his arms and the premature babies stamped his feet and shins with mouth-shaped globs of slobber, some suctioned to his skin like leeches. He expected to see the red premature baby, but it didn't appear. Yet, somehow, this made it more present.

He whispered to the baby suckling on his palm, *Where is he?* He wanted to be directed to the cryptic room where the premature baby hanged upside-down from a perch-shaped throne, enwrapped in rags, but he was greeted by silence punctuated with the salivation of lips, as if his arms and legs possessed nipples. *Where?* He looked up at the twisted crowd, their breaths escaping almost in the manner of the skeletal smoke. They, too, were silent. *Tell me… at once!* Peering into the faces of the premature babies at his feet and attached to him, he became dizzy by the portions of features he recognized. An insomniac eye there, a row of rotted teeth here. Light and dark. Sun and shade. Star and moon. *Begone!* He kicked them, tore them from his skin where they left impressions of teething. *Off I say!* The infant knights began to hack at the premature babies, lancing them from His Majesty's arms as though they were boils. And when the crowd remained silent, the infant king, covered in grisly residue, shouted, *Confess!* Only once the premature babies lay diced upon the ground, did the knights stop. The crowd wailed and, due to the white noise, the infant king was unsure of their true speech: *We don't know. Torture us. Save us. We know but won't tell. Kill us. Cure us.* The infant king filled the sky with his command, *Show yourself, you coward, show yourself! Tell me what you've done!* And the sounds of language collapsed, an implosion localized in the mud between the infant king's feet. He looked down, and there it was, a fire-wilted string of flesh, the remnant of his umbilical stump. Now he was only able to hear the trilling and festering cries of those afflicted. He raised two fists in the air. "B-buwn, buwn et aww!" Brandishing torches, the infant knights obeyed and set every shanty afire, and the infant king and Clovis rushed down the road and back to the castle, above which hung a round rock, textured like the very bones of the gods around them.

***

Baff toyme wuhs wun o' me fafoyite toymes. Wen me gawddess baffed me cuz I wuhs doyty et wuhs wike bein' unbown. Insoyde uh wittle washin' vessow, up ta me neck en wadduh, tickewd by uh pwefoah o' bubbews. She wood wub evewy pawt o' me boydy n' I wood cloyse me eyes n' be back insoyde o' me gawddess's bewwy. Sumtoymes she wood give me baff toys ta pway wit, uh wittle wooden duckwing, uh wittle wooden boyt, n' we wood boff make da soynds togefew: qwack, qwack, swosh, swosh. Wun o' da woyst toymes wuhs wen baff toyme wuhs ovuh. Et wuhs wike wewiving da howow o' bein' bown. I wood be powed fwom da wadduh, bweakin' thwew da spudded soyface, n' aw da wawmness wood dwip doyn me boydy. I wood cwy, but da gawddess wood hum ta me n' wap me en bwankets, howdin' me ta her boosom wike da baby I wuhs.

***

The infant king recalled the prophetic dream that had been sent to him during the climax of his slumber. He was racing an undersea chariot through thick and milky water toward an oval eclipse. All his competitors had been surpassed, but one. No matter how fiercely he whipped his foals, an ultimate rival remained adjacent, with the spearheaded hub of a wheel threatening to shred his spokes. When he had caught sight of the rival's face, he saw the premature baby, but with the features of adulthood. *Insofar as one is fixated on what the eyes see.* And those features, which he had perceived in isolation, scattered among the premature herd of the day before, resembled their father, the uncle. He had whiffed the treachery beforehand, tasted in the air a psychic energy belonging to a brewing coup, but had been unable to name it. And now he knew that the conspiring offspring's blood was composed of a distinct betrayal. He needed to find it, bring it and all those sympathizing traitors to justice. Yet it was the second part of the dream that had startled him awake so that his sobs required a silver pacifier provided by Clovis. His foals had perished mid-charge, and into the fleshy megalith the premature baby sped on, the absorption of which caused the structure to topple, the ruins rotting over the course of mere minutes.

In response to this revelation, the infant king ordered that the entire kingdom be baby-proofed. Among other precautions, all furniture was to be tied down with ropes, every corner and sharp edge blunted with cloth, chamber pots were to be emptied or covered with a wooden lid, and the cabinets of apothecaries and the like were to be locked. The infant king also decreed that pillows of any variety were forbidden, except for His Majesty's golden-threaded one, which was swollen with the fluff of a hundred goslings. Once confiscated, he had them all burned outside the castle walls, a conflagration that littered the air with singed wool, down, and cotton. The afternoon naps of that day resulted in sore necks and bizarre anxieties regarding sudden infant death syndrome. But, as if in pacification, the wealthiest citizens awoke to invitations for a celebratory banquet at the royal castle.

Never had the infant king felt safer in his new world, sitting at the head of the ever-long table in the banquet hall with the whole of his aristocracy at his mercy. His new pet, an albino lion cub, stretched at his feet, half-under the table, his glassy tail occasionally tickling the infant king's shins. Acquired from an infant merchant, His Majesty admired the translucent skin and thought that, in a way, this beast would wear his vulnerability for him, lay bare the fragile, twitching anatomy, but also protect him, for his claws were so delicate as to be invisible yet sharp enough to carve diamonds. His pink eyes, he knew, held both rage and affection.

Upon the table steamed whole peachicks, cygnets, and fetal herons, accompanied by loaves of bread, bowls of fava bean soup, piles of fish eggs drenched in yellow sauce, and marinated leeks in mustard vinaigrette. Exotic spices seasoned the ten-course meal, including saffron, cumin, nutmeg, cardamom, and cinnamon. Milk from his private cellar held warm in chalices. Before commencing the feast, the infant king pressed his navel and smirked as he felt the faint heat. Earlier in the day, after his dreamless nap, he had discovered something most auspicious. In the blackness of his bellybutton, an ember of light twinkled, providing enough psychic energy to eavesdrop on the entirety of the castle, his stone womb. He could hear the spiderlings weaving fragile webs, the clinking of counted treasure, the squealing squabs in the dovecotes, the haunted hum of the crypt, the clanking of spoons in boiling cauldrons, the splitting of light by the stained glass windows of the chapel, and praise-coated whispers over the patter of feet in the halls and bedchambers.

Amid jovial commotion, everyone washed their hands in bowls of water, and, once finished, the infant king stabbed a fork into the side of an apple-gagged piglet, thus quieting the hall. They stared at the silver handle of that utensil, then at the solemn infant king. His mouth trembled. Then he flailed his arms and giggled, a few saliva bubbles blowing from his mouth, and yelled, "Me woyaw soybchects. Be gwutinous!" Lively once more, the wealthy babies slurped, gnawed, sucked, and chomped. A few feet from the far end of the table, a performance began, which depicted the veritable story of His Majesty's divine birth: a midwife and a horn-headed uncle were played by infants on stilts. Upon a bed lay the infant king's mother, a baby girl whose head jutted from a dome-shaped wooden body. Toddlers dressed like birds were perched around the small stage, one atop the headboard, and began to sing in operatic voices, welcoming the parturition of a new age, a new king. Two quilted rainbows unfurled across the wall. Robed and crowned, a muscular toddler crawled without tears from the splintered womb. The midwife blew into a clarion while the newborn king stood and posed at the front of the stage, arms akimbo and dimpled chin held high. Black-dressed stagehands lit the uncle on fire, the blaze rushing up the stilts and enclosing the baby. He collapsed upon the ground, squirming and screaming. Some of the wealthy babies laughed and cheered, while others ceased eating, the burning body reflecting in their eyes. The smell evoked seared piglet. Portraying the warriors of far-off lands, infants on stilts surrounded the king, but he pushed them back with a sweeping motion of his hands. They cowered in fear of his supernatural power. Then, while white flowers rained upon the body of his mother in bed, stagehands tied a hanging rope around the king's waist and, arms open, he ascended into a hole in the sky-painted ceiling.

The clapping was gradual, but then became riotous, all the while the infant king smiled, his lips oiled with meat juices. After six minutes of constant clapping, the infant king raised his hands to end it. Servants brought more courses to the table, including rissoles and spiced quince butter cake. Infant dancers entered the hall and, as they pirouetted around the table to the alluring tune of the infant musicians, they removed garments of clothing. The wealthy babies cheered again before munching, licking, gurgling, and belching. The infant king tossed meat-draped bones beneath the table for his lion. When they had all finished eating, their bellies bulged and their clothes and mouths were stained and sticky. By then, the dancers were nearly nude, and the wealthy babies' lips instinctively began to pull in the direction of exposed nipples, their stubby fingers grabbing the air. It was at this juncture that the infant king's smile morphed into a lipless line. His eyes, the skin beneath them charcoaled, almost grew larger than his skull, and his crown was slumped forward and to the side. The infant dancers and musicians exited the hall. He brought up his golden rattle from under the table and, after holding it outward and horizontal for a moment, he dropped it onto his plate with an echoing clunk. Attempting to maintain nonchalance, the wealthy babies sniffed and wiped their mouths on their sleeves or on the damask tablecloths, while some used pointy bones to pick at tendrils of meat between their baby teeth. Clovis cleared his throat and produced a scrolled parchment. The babies looked at each other. Standing up, Clovis unrolled it and began to read, "Awfuw, Bwuno, Cheoffwey...." Infant knights appeared and dragged the named babies from their chairs. "Chawes, Gwegowy, Godfwey...." Deprived of language, the wealthy babies were reduced to infantile colic. More knights replaced those who left with the wriggling accused. The infant king remained slouched in his chair with his hand cupping his chin, his little finger pressing into his pale cheek, and whispered, "Fwow dem en da Cwib, fwow dem aw en da Cwib." "Cwistophe, Wowand, Coystanteen...." Fingering his navel, the infant king was able to translate the various cries as praises, supplications, and denunciations: *Long live the king! Many years for His Majesty! Please, no. I'm innocent. I don't want to die! Have mercy!* "Wéon, Mawcel, Maffias...." *Look to Philip, he has never known loyalty! Preposterous! It is Horace who has always leaned toward dissent! May His Majesty's kingdom reach to all four corners of the earth! I beg of thee!*

***

Not a purgatorial soul was allowed within the bedchamber of His Majesty now that all precautions were being heeded. This included the toddler advisor, and so a baby parrot in the capacity of messenger, perched on the rim of the infant king's basinet, relayed in a squawking voice Clovis' bedtime tale: Sum noyts, me mudda wood pway da fwoote, makin' such bootifew soynds, n' I wood go ta me fadda n' say, "Dada nahnahnahnahnuh." He wood wook doyn aht me wit his big moon face n' pick me up enta his skoy. Me mudda wood pway fasta n' he wood swing me awound suh quickwy dat me awms n' wegs wood feew stwetched oyt, me face uhs big uhs da gawds! I wood see da wowd fwom deir gweat height, n' eweyting ewse wood feew suh smaw. I nevah wanted ta go back doyn dere. But da gawds wood eventuawy tiwuh of da pwayin' n' da dancin' n' I wood be smaw again n' no mattew how many toymes I sed, "Dada nahnahnahnahnuh nahnahnahnahnuh," it woodn't change uh ting, cuz dey wood awedy be goyne.

* * *

There were multitudinous rumors surrounding the Crib. Many imagined that interrogations were facilitated by racks, brazen calves, breaking wheels, toe wedging, head crushers, and flagellations. Some said the dank dungeon was infested with rat pups, pink and transparent. Huddled together like intestines, the vermin would awaken on impulse and, starting at the feet, gnaw lethargically on the chained prisoners. Whatever did or did not occur within the Crib, one occasion was to be immortalized with a public viewing: the executions of the accused.

The infant king had slept long and well during the night and into the day, knowing that his loyal torturers would extract the pertinent information. He awoke to the baby parrot's chirping, followed by a briefing on four contradictory confessions obtained from within the Crib: the premature baby had retreated to the mountains, surviving in a cave and learning the ways of bears; admiring statistics and infinities, the premature baby had become a star and, no matter how many His Majesty destroyed, it would live forever, implementing esoteric optics to communicate with its followers; mastering the spells of a black book, the premature baby had committed suicide so that its liberated soul could occupy any open-mouthed body at will; made of replicative flesh, the premature baby had severed its thumb, pinky, and index finger, thus growing three clones to occupy the other corners of the earth so that it could evade capture and have time to plan its coochie coochie coup. The baby parrot then croaked that experts, including toddler geographers, astronomers, philosophers, and alchemists, were devising relevant solutions to each possibility.

Now, sitting in his royal tent at a safe distance from the eager crowd, the infant king had the finest view of the dozen nooses that hung from a long beam, slowly spinning or swaying by the breeze. The moon, that calcified eye, shone with a misty light and affected the surrounding torches with a bruised hue. On this night, all his fears would be mollified. He smiled as he thought, How effective is a coup without traitors? More than this, he longed for when he could relish in the news that the premature baby had been hunted down, regardless of whatever form it took. If it had mimicked the bears, he would keep it as his groveling pet, a plaything for his lion. If it had become a star, he would pull it down from the sky and entrap the iridescent dot as his crown jewel. If it were a measly soul, he would consume it, effortlessly digested by his stomach acid. If four of it existed, he would hang their lacerated corpses from the earth's corners, tassels to his future kingdom. None would dare threaten him, the infinite infant, the eternal king.

The crowd cheered as the foal-pulled wagons arrived, stuffed with the accused, their bare bodies wounded. Some with the kisses of a whip between their shoulder blades, others with limbs seemingly soldered back together. One baby bore the stigmata like a shrunken martyr. Infant knights kept the crowd at bay while the executioner led the prisoners to their respective stools, beneath the nooses. Their faces were passive, as though their tear ducts had been cauterized. Such stoicism bothered the infant king, but when the executioner looked to him, he nodded.

The executioner hollered, "His Machesty has decweed n' given sentoynce dat aw twaitors shaw be coyndemned fwom wife n' hung undil deaf dof ensue."

One by one, he fitted the nooses around each baby's neck. The infant king sipped from his chalice of milk and was disappointed to find it had cooled. He poured some into his lion's golden bowl and heard the subsequent lapping as the sound of gratitude. The infant king looked down and could see the liquid cascade through the lion's throat and slosh in his stomach.

Standing by the first prisoner, the executioner asked them

all, "Eny wast wowds?"

A dozen silent babies, statues to their own fleeting memory. The infant king craved to hear their confessions, especially from those who had given nothing in the Crib. This was the moment in which all their spying and scheming should be vomited forth as sin-laden babble. He gulped his milk and shook his rattle. "Wat say yuh!"

Donning the middle noose, the stigmata'd baby began to laugh, a kind of crow cackling. The crowd looked to the baby then to the infant king, wondering how he would respond. The other eleven prisoners began to laugh, a hysterical chorus. The infant king tapped his bellybutton, waited, then tapped it again, then again. The laughter seemed as contagious as the plague and he imagined everyone had begun emitting such sounds, including himself. He tapped it once more, he fingered it, nearly puncturing the shimmering film of psychic skin, but the laughter was untranslatable, meaningless yet threatening. "Siwence!"

The executioner kicked away the first stool and the hanged baby twitched and writhed, toes reflexively spreading. As the infant king witnessed this punishment, he felt as if his own neck were being strangled, and dropped his chalice, the clanging sound muted by the uproar. Was this a poison taking hold in him, slowly constricting his airways? Then the executioner fell before he could kick the second stool, and two, four, six cloaked infants pushed through the crowd, wielding poniards. The noosed babies shouted, "Fweedom! Joystice! Wibewation!" Before the assassins could reach the steps to His Majesty's throne, his pet lion charged forward, releasing a viscid roar, and slashed them. Most of the panicked crowd fled or took cover. After nearly disemboweling a fallen assassin, the lion sank his teeth into the neck of another, and a music began to play, composed of fluid and resonant chords, such a sweet melody. As the lion ripped out a trachea, it slumped to the ground, sleeping, its chin resting in the blood-filled cavity of the infant's neck. The remaining assassins stabbed the lion in the leg, heart, paw, and head. The infant king saw his knights standing still. He couldn't command them. He tried to shake his rattle but the poison must have had a paralyzing effect. The music stopped and Clovis came around the curtains of the tent and entered, a lute in one hand and a sword in the other. He dropped the lute and its strings quaked. He lifted the sword, pulling it back so that its tip pointed at the infant king's navel.

"Yuh too, Cwoyvis?"

With a sheen in his eyes, Clovis hesitated, then plunged the sword as far as it could go. Blood ejected from the infant king's mouth and he became numb from the chest down. Beginning at the back of his head, he felt formication on his skin, but no, it was the nailless fingers he had once heard scuttling across the stony floor of his throne room, and those fingers cupped his chin, pulling his head back, and he saw the looming figure of the premature baby, raising high a blade whittled from his pillow-wielding uncle's metacarpal. The infant king found himself justified, without doubt or compunction, because, indeed, an assassin had been in their midst, the heir to an avuncular usurper, the prenatal voice of the people, the self-proclaimed alpha and omega, but all of that dissipated, and in a throat-slit death throe the sharp steel in his stomach became his abandoned umbilical cord, reconnecting him to his divine mother, whose merciful face floated above, singing, *Mon trésor, mon John, sombre dans un profond sommeil…*

Three Poems

Jesse Glass

The Man With The Tiny Penis

walked a strong dog named Weakness
down a side street that opened into
a National Highway.

Did he live without thinking?
He tried his best, my Capitano,
and when he ate supper it was from
antiquest Tupperware. His dog was so worn
it offered no resistance to sunshine
or Sorocco. Not one firefly could hide in its eviscerated shadow,
nor could a real flea batten on imaginary blood
from the constant garden of its loins.

No one had pity for his situation.
Not the old man creeping forth like a rat-faced baby,

nor the young woman with dirty hair
who sold used lottery tickets to the homeless,

nor would the long-sufferers in hospices
(between bouts of majong and paint-by-numbers)
stop their death-ward progression to consider his condition.

He is saving his pennies in an old jam jar
for a nameless operation
that will lift him quite out of himself
like religion or literature
& shore him up in the presence
of the more generously endowed.

(LATER)
He died on the operating table.
This is no joke. He died
trying to levitate after drinking too much cough medicine
in a Neo-Gothic building by a 7-11.
We forget *certain details*. He became something of a god in the tabloids
& is remembered chiefly for his blustering manner and his delicate hands.
We cast his mournful visage in bronze
& erected his stainless steel stele in the shade of a monumental Dog
cut from a single block of Chinese marble. His epitaph: **BE ABOUT TO DO.**

Traveler's Song

Cold, is,
a, h,a,m,m,e,r, in, my, throat,
forehead, aches,
eyes, water,
cars,
roll, by, my, n,u,m,b,f,o,o,t, stagger,
withered, thumb,
points, to Z,e,r,o,
moon-dark, light, on,
brittle, shoulders.
along, this, highway,
a,p,p,a,l,o,o,s,a,'d, with ice,
clouds, rise, like,
auto-medicated, breath.
where, can, I, go,
without, falling, asleep,
with my, j,e,w,e,l,s
in, my, left, hand:
an, o,f,f,e,r,l,n,g, to, d,e,a,t,h?

Songs for the Unwashed Ka-Billions

1.

"Spotter Planes Were Last Seen Searching…"

for Venus thumb-tacked to a Catherine's Wheel, foregrounded
against intersections of stained glass slats,
bubbled surfaces, (inter-bang & alia)-greased

barbells for arms against the sparks
head a spent rifle cartridge
redolent of explosions in *R-Town*;

her four mystic smears
lever debrided skies. Breasts
pierced by phantom shrikes, regulus
fluttering up-flue: she decamps

coagulant, brilliant, into estrus

where nothing is; her instant an excised
breath caught in ladles of horn & pearl

before Love's scissor shape
leveled the white caps into
grainy progressions worthy of Heraclitean gandy-dancers dripping

glittery facts for dodderers, she rode—no surfed—no dimpled--the meniscus—
to siphonophoric applause
& gracefully assaulted our collective Eye
rolling in morphew.

2.

"In Edinburgh, everything's made of atoms, I think…"*

so is there a reason for dabbling in gift shop after-
shave? Or unpacking the implied Carlyle-isms—Thomas' and Jane's
from the "Highland Temblor" as it was danced morosely three seconds ago
in the shadow of Hume Tower for a busload of "lost American cousins 'cumin' hayme'"?
Or striking a conga drum with a jumble of rusted gears before taking flight
via refurbished Montgoflier, then stripping the gores away just to the right of
a T. O' Shanter sunset to gusts of applause
and managing the plunge
with no visible release of spring-loaded, revolutionary pamphlets
& barely a screaming allusion to the Athens of the North's

long enragement with Descartes? Pascal? Leibniz? Reid's canny book of answers

crowns with no true equivalent
the fly's ontological escapades when rendering to chowder
pigmented orts tweezed from Scottish Nat'l Gallery noses, so
that it "knows at least what the 'twa corbies' knew
among the midden heaps on the shores of AWLD Reekie"--
an irregular assertion empirically unbound—
but waiting for the trowel and the test-pit prayers of Hugh Miller nevertheless
and so conclude that the negating of these trans-gringo-Gongorisms could mean even less
than a squalid, lattice-eyed
Truth latent in the Caledonian earth, for aye.

*--Democritus, Jr.

3.

Extra! Extra!

After eating a box of chicken nuggets at ground zero

We'd found our Authentic Voice and the ability to project lead into gold with an imported vial
Of Saint Dunstan's red powder. "It's just a trick of memory, mercury and ma…mirrors.

we recall stutt-shouttering among the bamboo groves of Nagasaki Peace Park
over our shoulders to photo-sharks who followed us everywhere, lenses focused but dropped--,
then lifted again in eternal fascination at our conjectures on the nature of revulsion
within choo choo distance of the old Scot's 'Grubber Gardens' and his revolutionary house.
We didn't pout or cry as many do, when told that God is a broken belt buckle
Lodged & rusting in Spunkenheimer's ear canal; we didn't quail when discovering that the EVENT
Was nothing less than some whistled Bach rising to meet a rapidly falling object of steel
& authentic pop-riveted beauty
intoning its own tubas in the diminishing distance above 70,000 collective heads and it,
and then everything suddenly
dancing dancing dancing with the aplomb
of the girls in the "Mysterious Voynich Manuscript"
entwined in Beddoes slippers & Faraday cages for hat or helmet, alchemical as hoot:
then given old go-go boots & mini-skirts borrowed from a Logical Positivist's conception of Twiggy
nude between the book marks, Cokes lifted to burnt-off lips
crepe-paper flames pinned to breasts & shoulders. We didn't stamp our penny-loafers
& demand that the everyday world be restored to Asian sensitivities
& that truth tables render up truths that could be applied equally to sunburn or chagas disease.
"What was it that really happened here, sensei?" the small voices asked.
And I, for the rest of the night, tried to tell them

to tell them. And so did the thundering meteor-headed-owls known as Tengu

to tell them. As the T,e,n,g,u told.

4.

…silver bead shot into steel blossom
distends into singing Orphic head
captured on video by two teen-aged girls via I-phone
at a boyfriend's wake ('died tragically young' a given) & is in turn
made available on hand-held DEVICES to the Ka-billions
who tweet tokens of belief or dis in

REAL TIME
(REAL TIME
REAL TIME
ETC.)

To the Giggling, Middle-Aged Host:
Destined for sex scandal before heart-attack
Threw him head forward face down on macadam
Tears running mercury beads

Back to the nearest bodega

Applause applause applause at his MYSTERY WIDE SHOW
Aired precisely at O-bon

We know

that
mirrors grant hasty wings
to butterflies, ok
torn in 2
by late-flowering punks on a lark

(afire to patch in the word 'quantum' with anything to grant relevance)

our wondering hamiletic crew crowded in aura of tantrum
searching out sources of angst by torchlight
among the synchronized swimming teams
set loose on the RED QUANTUM SEA awash alack bones still
scabby with radiation sickness

Still,
One T.V. camera trained on another
by an Anglican Theosophist
at the end of a final talk show evening bonanza
gives a 'PRETTY ACCURATE' picture of eternity according to the crowd of Jesuit

Adventurers raised on ground beef
pressed into patties
by secret process.

…and 'Shogun' reruns

There's a quietus coming this way to your world too
& we'll administer it, when we're damned ready to, ok?
& we'll administer it
All over this land. It won't be pretty to do or see
& it won't have
One hint of heroism about it
But it will be precise, timely & apt
Because we insist on saying so.

5.

Shhh! (Whispering) It's called Japonisme, but that's all I really want to say about
The elephant in the room that always flits

Thru this country of multilingual discussionists. First there's the Hieroglyphanist
And her husband the physicist, who doubles as a pianist

For a really swinging gang of Jazz bangers on his nights off from the lab
(O Pretend you're a Cycladic sculpture ('s flowing plane for a face) to estab-

Lish your entailment to the nuance of these precisionists!—yet go on aging as if none

Of this mattered to any old punter—you long gone gong struck by a Zen Nun

Parentheses cut in the air thereby and filled with a vibrating surfeit of clangorous memory,)
The next—nobody's heroine—a virago (trilingual) queen of the foreigners' plenary

Returned to become the secretary of a small cement company. Summarily fired. "Will you?..."
She dryly requested, before she shed her tiara and boarded the Airbus to L.A. & flew

With hopes of ruling at least one valve of the American heart, (j-husband now deftly abandoned).
Her 'I'm so respected & special' destined to go up in flames as soon as she returns to the land

Of minimum wage and shrugs for the likes of late middle-aged freckly Divas like her,
sporting a Phi Beta Kappa for her dance major M.A., by the way! And the conversational vigor

She turns like a gun on every puzzled interviewer—"Keep in touch," she said, offering her hand
To all the members of the foreigners society of Chiba-ken, where she ruled her 'jolly band'

Helping desperate hot-line callers way into the night, who couldn't abide the nuanced culture,
Protecting belly dancers, bar girls and exchange students from the vultures

Who wouldn't accommodate the sensitivities (or the proclivities) of a poor lady from—Texas—say,
Or any of the lower 48, come to explore the land of the Rising Sun and then go away

prejudices unruffled. She was paid well too and gave ballet lessons to further engorge

Her prestige, her purse & her now estranged husband's credit line, (his hello j-name 'George')

But back to our consideration of failed Oxonian Thespians, lost Romanian gymnastics teachers
Writers of English haiku and destitute Russian researchers

Of physics, German biologists, Australian philosophers looking for more than a stipend
In Kangaroo hell now teaching conversational English to those primed to send

Their charmingly cultured children abroad—knucklehead economists,--back-pack journalists
Film-makers, college drop-outs turned "gifted raconteurs" and don't forget fetal industrialists

How you all go on and on and on as the butterfly's wing tips the O'd rings
Of the ode and epode of the rhapsode that is alien you, & of your Western brilliance sings—

How your abandoned lumps of meat stink & fade, your common little gifts, your bright yesterdays
A trail of dried jazz and coffee-clatch odor and imprecise memories close to lies, but not quite

From how you got here to where you finally got off, & most definitely GOT YOURS,
Shhhh! & Good night!

Carol Watts' Poetry

Kelptown (Shearsman, 2020)

A Time of Eels (Oystercatcher, 2021)

Toby Olson

The mysteries of the natural world, as viewed mostly on and below the sea's surface, and our place in it, which is also a mystery, is the major subject of Carol Watts' remarkable poetry. How does one confront these mysteries?

> you say *I have not seen*
> *a more beautiful field*
>
> as if the compliment
> should give you entry
>
> land unresponsive a skate
> boned out to air. . .

This unresponsiveness is often echoed in human relations, mysterious for the reader, but clear for the speaker, as the workings of the natural world are clear in that foreign realm.

The way the word became unarmed.
The way a blow to the head became a blow
to the heart, how cruelty warps the tongue.

Yet the forest grows up and us woven in it,
already fathoms down and singing cellular
where the ground once was, and our words

for world migrating. . . .

Half way through *Kelptown* and its variety, one comes upon a series named "T.R.E.E. (Total Rare Earth Elements)," which was "prompted by a phrase from Jackson Mac Low's 'It is a Simple Life,'" and here Watts works with the sentence and what properties it might reveal. The poems are, for the most part, straight forward syntactically, but for the simple, yet powerful, technique whereby slashes are used, much in the way Mac Low used them, to isolate phrases, thus pushing forward added significance within sentences. There is a narrative developed in these eight poems, and, given the slashes, there are many additional narratives. Here's an example, the third poem in this series:

small inhalings / would have protected for centuries / without
surgical intervention / this daily / life / inter / venes / the hawk
adjusts / the marshes were close by / but there was a clarity / it is
too late for / me / words / have talked their way / so superficial when
/ such violence / obtains / I think what is next / where do I / walk
/ what jetty extends / silence / no do I walk / this jetty / because
something / will follow / I / take it in to myself / this jetty is/ on
my tongue / is / my tongue / I hurried elsewhere yet / what was
in my bones / is repeated close to the skull / look look / a pale light
/ I was born into this / uh-o uh-oh / I do regret not seeing you /
while you knew / asking / what a move / I must learn to 'take it in' /

There are moments in the poems in *Kelptown* that, for the most part, dispense with the mysteries of the natural world in exchange for the autobiographical:

A system of ties, and the way the body shows
it metre unbidden. I woke up with bruises. . . .

Still the power of this book rests in engagement with those
natural phenomenons that are mostly ignored in our daily lives.
Watts insists that we not turn away from what's beyond us, those
complexities that are at least as complex as our own personal
histories and human concerns. We might see ourselves as a part of
nature, but Watts sees nature as apart from us, foreign and elegant,
and unconcerned, and this attitude is beautifully displayed in her
fifteen-poem sequence *A Time of Eels.*

Marsyas is a lonely hover

a long red pipe. . .

The haunting strains of Arvo Part's *Lamentate*, presented in
honor of Anish Kapoor's *Marsyas*, a monumental abstract sculpture
installed at the Tate Modern in London, suggests the sounds
produced by Marsyas himself, that mythological Satyr who was said
to have invented the music of the flute. A long red pipe, an image
of Kapoor's sculpture, as well as the shape of an eel. This and the
glow worm caves in New Zealand, provide the context for these
remarkable poems. As there is a massive eel in the Tate Modern,
there is an eel too in the cave of lights. Here is the second poem in
the series:

you are here
I did not expect to find you

here how soft this dark
when lanterns shut

I begin stooping in sound
as if the roof descends

long threads in suspension
spun cadences are

poison filaments snaring
any thing venturing out

by air memories not buried
but matters of collision

float unseen until light
picks out a thousand

points of capture minutes
from your face yet

these dimensions are the same
the cave is the same

All avant guard movements question existing practice, then their arguments find their way into future poetries. It might be argued that Carol Watts' writing has taken the philosophy of the Language movement seriously, then built upon it to produce a powerful poetry that is all her own. One need only look at Watts' *A Time of Eels* to see the beautiful fruits of this engagement.

Telling Time: Rosemarie Waldrop's
The Nick of Time
(New Directions, 2021)

John Olson

I think of knuckles when I read Rosmarie Waldrop's work, and
nuts. Knuckles because of their superb articulation, their synovial
and cartilaginous intermeshing, their finesse and flexibility. And
nuts because nuts are nuts: a palpable pericarp around a kernel
of postulation. It's easy to make metaphors out of Waldrop's work
because the work confers the power of metaphor-making. Waldrop's
language is one informed by Stein and Wittgenstein: everything is
always a proposal, always a syncopation, a shift in meaning, so that
meaning is expanded to mean language itself, its propagation and
fertility, its discrepancies and coalescences, its suspicious celerity
and dreamlike clarity.

The Nick of Time is a collection of prose poetry. It's
divided into ten sections with individual poems – laments to poets,
contemporaries and former friends, who have passed – sandwiched
between. The individual prose poems are modest in size, 200 to 300
words, whose block-like appearance on the page confers a sense
of materiality on them. The tone is meditative and philosophical and
reminds me a little of Thomas Traherne's *Centuries of Meditations*
in their contemplative warmth and occasional spiritual undertones;
present, too, like a woodwind instrument making itself known

during the quieter intervals of a symphony is Ludwig Wittgenstein's *Philosophical Investigations*, those rather austere little paragraphs examining – in deceptively simple terms - the nature of language and how it informs and shapes consciousness.

The Nick of Time reads like a book of light and shadow. Its two chief preoccupations – language and time – emerge and remerge in different registers and contexts, syntactically reenacting "the overlapping of successive perceptions in the cortex" ["Perseverance"]. Waldrop mingles – quite seamlessly – the quotidian with the metaphysical, the larger concerns running in the deeper waters of our existence, our *Seinsfrage*, our continual questioning of the nature of Being. Waldrop's collection is fundamentally a poetic embroidery patterned on the ontology of existence, a textual brocade threaded with the spirit of rumination that flourishes in old age when short term memory weakens and long term memory grows freakishly introspective in its breadth and scope. If this sounds a bit pretentious or stuffy, it's not. Not at all. This is an eminently readable language. The sentences tend to be short, oftentimes a litany of single words, whose dispersal is rendered with great delicacy and skill.

If we think of language as the shadow of a higher, more intense reality than the fingers of light agitating on a coffee table on a sunny afternoon, or the seraphim of clouds mimicking the processes of thought on some vast western horizon, then language potentiates its most metaphysical aspect, which is to underscore the very phenomena for which – by its very function as a substitute for what isn't there – it creates an absence. And in the hands of a poet like Rosmarie Waldrop that's precisely the effect the language attains: it quietly unravels its discoveries in a continuous present, "like the cat that rubs her chin along your leg. Or Gertrude Stein. Or like that distant waking. Into light made complex by cherry branches cutting across it. So many leaf edges. Spread as widely as the phenomena of thinking." ["Asymmetry"].

Note the fragmentation in the above excerpt. This is similar to a strategy Stein occasionally employed in pieces such as "How She Bowed To Her Brother," "Grant Or Rutherford B. Hayes," "Winning His Way" and other pieces, in which sentences are broken up into fragments that interrupt the flow and focus attention on the structures of perception and language. When Stein writes "And now everybody. Reads. She bowed. To her brother," we stumble and pause and our attention is heightened by the irregularity of the rhythm. If we reassemble it in a conventional manner, "And now everybody reads. She bowed to her brother," the perception is speeded up but the focus is blurred by the ordinariness of the syntax. It's such a simple effect, but it goes a long way toward emphasizing the carpentry behind meaning, the gaps behind joints for ventilation.

The third section of "The Almost Audible Passing Of Time" blends Waldrop's dual fascination with language and time in a single small block of prose that seems larger than it is because of the range of its references and the scope of its proposals.

> Ritual, repetition, rhyme. For centuries we've tried to thwart the arrow. But even when, at the prayer of Joshua, the Sun stood still, time nevertheless continued. Likewise when Rousseau tossed his watch. Staring at the mottled bark of the sycamore, do I think this ritual will protect me from the constant changes of my body? The run toward dust to dust? Is it to freeze this moment before the mosquitos come with their cargo of itches that I watch beetles and weeds and pods, as if I were interested in them? But I don't even know their name – when words and their entanglements are my feelers. Without them I'm in darkness.

The arrow to which Waldrop refers is the arrow of time, the illusion that time has a forward momentum carrying us from the past to the future. And between the past and the future is the present, which is also an illusory phenomenon. "There is our past," observes theoretical physicist Carlo Rovelli,

> ...all the events that happened before what we can witness now. There is our future: the events that will happen after the moment from which we can see the here and now. Between this past and this future there is an interval that is neither past nor future and still has a duration: fifteen minutes on Mars; eight years on Proxima b; millions of years in the Andromeda galaxy. It is perhaps the greatest and strangest of Einstein's discoveries.
>
> The idea that a well-defined now exists throughout the universe is an illusion, an illegitimate extrapolation of our

own experience.

It is like the point where the rainbow touches the forest. We think that we can see it – but if we go to look for it, it isn't there.

Given the anguish that accompanies aging and its inevitable consequence, it's only natural to turn to language as the medium that will freeze it. But it doesn't really freeze anything. There is anguish in the story of Joshua's prayer to God to make the sun to stand still, and there is anguish in Rousseau's gesture of tossing his watch, as if shooting a clock with a .357 Magnum would end the progression of time. Time is as maddeningly elusive as it is unstoppable. Waldrop's comparison of words to insect feelers is apt: thinking produces heat in our heads, and that heat feeds on the agitation of molecules. Words like antennal sensilla are wonderful, but not everything that can be thought can be said, said Wittgenstein. "Even mislaid," Waldrop writes, "time burns at both ends, and my body no longer moves with the energy of electrons through longitudes, latitudes. And in altitudes I get sick. My face tells the time without wheels or springs moving inside the brain."

Notes on Contributors

Charles Bernstein's recent books included *Topsy-Turvy* (Chicago, 2021) and *Pitch of Poetry* (Chicago, 2016). He is the winner of the 2019 Bollingen Prize for *Near/Miss* (University of Chicago Press, 2018) and for lifetime achievement in American Poetry. He was born in 1950 in Manhattan and now lives in Brooklyn.

Ian Brinton's most recent publications include *Language and Death*, a translation of poems by Philippe Jaccottet (Equipage, 2022), Paul Valéry's *Selected Poems* (Preface by Michael Heller), Muscaliet Press, 2021, *Paris Scenes*, a translation of Baudelaire's 'Tableaux Parisiens', Two Rivers Press, 2021 and *Islands of Voices*, selected poems of Douglas Oliver (Shearsman Books, 2020). He reviews for *The London Magazine, PN Review, Litter, Long Poem Magazine* and *Golden Handcuffs Review*; he co-edits the magazine *SNOW*.

Lee Duggan's first collection, *Reference Points* (Aquifer 2017) met with enthusiastic reviews in *Poetry Wales, Elliptical Movements,* and *Litter Magazine.* Her highly individual sonnet sequence *Green* (Oystercatcher 2019) was also met with critical acclaim. Lee's work featured in the ground breaking anthology of contemporary Welsh innovative poetry, *The Edge of Necessary* (Aquifer 2018). More recently her work has appeared in *Tentacular, Tears in the Fence, Noon, Molly Bloom, Poetry Wales* and *Junction Box.* She has forthcoming collections from Aquifer, Knives, Forks and Spoons, and Contraband. She is based on the northern outskirts of Snowdonia.

Norman Fischer is a poet, essayist and Soto Zen Buddhist priest who has written and published steadily since the late 1970's. Recent poetry titles include *Nature, There Was A Clattering As..., The Museum of Capitalism,* and *Selected Poems 1980-2013.* His *Experience: On Thinking, Writing, Language and Religion* was published in the University of Alabama Press Poetics Series in 2016. His latest Buddhist title is *When You Greet Me I Bow: Notes and Reflections from a Life in Zen.* He lives in Muir Beach CA with his wife Kathie, also a Zen priest.

Nancy Gaffield is the author of six poetry publications, including *Meridian* (Longbarrow Press 2019), *Continental Drift* (Shearsman 2014), and *Tokaido Road* (CB editions 2011). She adapted *Tokaido Road* into a libretto; the opera, composed by Nicola LeFanu, premiered at the Cheltenham Music Festival in 2014 before touring the UK in 2015. She has also published three chapbooks, including most recently *Wealden*, which explores the consonance between nature, poetry and electronic music (www.longbarrwpress.com). She is an honorary academic in Creative Writing at the University of Kent, and co-edits the online magazine: *Free Verse: A Journal of Contemporary Poetry & Poetics.*

Jesse Glass' poetry will be featured in Jessica Lewis Luck's *Poetics of Cognition: Thinking Through Experimental Poems* from the University of Iowa Press later this year. A section of his long poem exploring the contexts of the death of the Westminster, Maryland Civil War editor Joseph Shaw in April 1865 appeared in *Gargoyle Magazine #74.*

Ralph Hawkins has two books appearing this year, *Trumpets Stuffed With Cloth* from Crater Press and *A Fancy Breeze Gets Up* from Shearsman. Shearsman also republished his 1981 volume, *Tell Me No More and Tell* in 2021. He is also a visual artist and has worked in collaborations with Alan Halsey and Kelvin Corcoran and with Bob Cobbing.

Fanny Howe has written novels and poetry and essays, many from Graywolf Press.

Pierre Joris just published his *Celebratory Talk-Essay on Receiving the Batty Weber Award* (CNL, Literary Talks series), *Fox-trails, -tales & -trots* (poems & proses, Black Fountain Press); in 2020 he completed his 1/2 century Celan translation project with *Memory Rose into Threshold Speech: The Collected Earlier Poetry of Paul Celan* (FSG) & *Microliths: Posthumous Prose of Paul Celan* (Contra Mundum Press). Also in 2020, *A City Full of Voices: Essays on the Work of Robert Kelly* (CMP) & in 2019, *Arabia (not so) Deserta* (essays, Spuyten Duyvil) & *Conversations in the Pyrenees* with Adonis (CMP). Forthcoming fall 2022 from CMP are *Always the Many, Never the One: Conversations in-between*, with Florent Toniello & *Interglacial* (Poems 1915-2020).

Hank Lazer's most recent books of poems are *When the Time Comes* (Dos Madres Press) and *field recordings of mind in morning* (BlazeVOX), which includes 15 tracks of musical improvisations (available on Bandcamp and YouTube) with composer and banjo player Holland Hopson. Lazer has published thirty-one prior books of poetry, including *COVID 19 SUTRAS, Slowly Becoming Awake (N32), Poems That Look Just Like Poems,* and *Thinking in Jewish (N20)*. Forthcoming soon from BlazeVOX is *P I E C E S*, a book-length poem in fragments. See Lazer's website: https://www.hanklazer.com

Stacey Levine's books are *The Girl with Brown Fur: Tales and Stories, Frances Johnson* (a novel), *Dra--* (a novel), and *My Horse and Other Stories.* Her short fiction has been translated into Danish and Japanese. Her novel *Mice 1961* will be published soon.

Brian Marley was once a poet, of sorts. His recent books are *Apropos Jimmy Inkling,* a novel, and a volume of short fiction, *The Shenanigans.* He and Ken Edwards run Grand Iota, a small publishing house that nurtures and disseminates adventurous prose writing. His current projects are *Crime, My Destiny*, a palimpsest novel, and *SELF[ish]*, which consists of 50 miniature stories coupled with 50 self-portraits, in both of which the author is, for want of a better word, abstracted.

John Olson is the author of numerous books of poetry and prose poetry, including *Weave of the Dream King, Dada Budapest, Larynx Galaxy,* and *Backscatter: New and Selected Poems*. He has also published five novels, including *The Seeing Machine, In Advance of the Broken Justy, The Nothing That Is, Mingled Yarn,* and *Souls of Wind*, which was shortlisted for a Believer Book of the Year Award in 2008.

Toby Olson's most recent volume is, *Journeys On A Dime*, his selected stories (Grand Iota). He is currently working on both stories and poems.

Kat Peddie is a lecturer in Creative Writing at the University of Kent. Publications include *Spaces for Sappho* (Oystercatcher 2016) and the digital opera *The Octopus* (composed by Lauren Redhead, Pan y Rosas Discos 2020) and poems and photographs published in *Tears in the Fence, Shearsman Magazine, Snow, Tentacular, Datableed, Golden Handcuffs Review, Litmus, Molly Bloom* and *Junction Box*, among others. These poems are from a projected collection *The Lives of the Artists.* She performs regularly with the music, dance & performance collective Free Range and is one half of a band, Kate's Bush, that produces mainly Poet's Theatre-esque plays.

George Salis is the author of the novel *Sea Above, Sun Below*, which was praised by Alexander Theroux and Rikki Ducornet. He's also the editor of *The Collidescope*, an online publication that celebrates innovative and neglected literature. His fiction is featured in *The Dark, Black Dandy, Sci Phi Journal, Three Crows Magazine*, and elsewhere. His criticism has appeared in *Isacoustic, Atticus Review,* and *The Tishman Review*, and his science article on the mechanics of natural evil was featured in *Skeptic*. For about the past 5 years, he has been working on a maximalist novel titled *Morphological Echoes*. He has taught in Bulgaria, China, and Poland.

Since he last appeared in *Golden Handcuffs*, **Ron Silliman** has had poetry in *Poetry, The Paris Review, Ariadne,* and *Fence*.

Michael Spafford was born in Palm Springs, California, in 1935 and grew up in Southern California. He received a BA from Pomona College in 1959, followed by a MA from Harvard University in 1960. He moved with his wife, artist Elizabeth Sandvig, to Mexico City in 1960, where he lived and worked before accepting a position to teach art and art history at the University of Washington in 1963. Professor Emeritus since 1994, he was an active and influential member of the Seattle arts community. Spafford showed with Francine Seders Gallery from 1966 until the gallery closed in 2013. He continued to paint and exhibit up until his death.

Spafford used Greco-Roman mythology as the catalyst for a body of work spanning 60 years, using the myths as avenues of expression about contemporary culture. He continually found new inspiration and perspectives for fresh imagery, resulting in extended series for The Labors of Hercules, the *Iliad*, the *Odyssey*, and mythologies surrounding Europa, and Romulus and Remus.

Spafford's honors and awards include a Louis Comfort Tiffany Foundation Grant in 1966 and Rome Prize Fellowships in 1967 and 1968; a King County Arts Commission's Honors Award, 1979; an Art Award from the American Academy and Institute of Arts and Letters, 1983; and the first Neddy Artist Fellowship from The Behnke Foundation in 1996. In 2005, he was invited to be Artist-In-Residence at Dartmouth College which included a major exhibition of recent paintings. He was honored with Lifetime Contribution to Northwest Art Award (shared with wife Elizabeth Sandvig) in 2017.

His website, www.michaelspafford.com, remains active.

Habib Tengour was born in 1947 in Mostaganem, Eastern Algeria and has lived most of his life between Algeria and Paris. He is the author of over fifteen books of poetry, essays, and drama. He directs the series Poems of the World, published by APIC in Algiers. His work available in English translation includes *"Exile is my Trade": The Habib Tengour Reader*, edited and translated by Pierre Joris, and *Crossings*, translated by Marilyn Hacker. With Pierre Joris, he edited *Poems for the Millennium, Volume Four: The University of California Book of North African Literature*.

www.ingramcontent.com/pod-product-compliance
Lightning Source LLC
Chambersburg PA
CBHW072003170626
46813CB00005B/1988